G R JORDAN

Cleared to Die

A Highlands and Islands Detective Thriller

*This book was professionally typeset on Reedsy.
Find out more at reedsy.com*

All human life can be found in an airport

DAVID WALLIAMS

Contents

Foreword

The Isle of Mull has an airstrip used for General Aviation flights and also for vital air ambulance services to the island. In this novel I have made the airfield and facilities more akin to the island airports of Stornoway, Shetland and Kirkwall with a full air traffic control unit and scheduled flights several times a day to other Scottish airports.

Acknowledgement

To Ken, Jessica, Jean, Colin, Susan and Rosemary for your work in bringing this novel to completion, your time and effort is deeply appreciated.

Novels by G R Jordan

The Highlands and Islands Detective series (Crime)

1. Water's Edge
2. The Bothy
3. The Horror Weekend
4. The Small Ferry
5. Dead at Third Man
6. The Pirate Club
7. A Personal Agenda
8. A Just Punishment
9. The Numerous Deaths of Santa Claus
10. Our Gated Community
11. The Satchel
12. Culhwch Alpha
13. Fair Market Value
14. The Coach Bomber
15. The Culling at Singing Sands
16. Where Justice Fails
17. The Cortado Club
18. Cleared to Die
19. Man Overboard!

Kirsten Stewart Thrillers (Thriller)

1. A Shot at Democracy
2. The Hunted Child
3. The Express Wishes of Mr MacIver
4. The Nationalist Express
5. The Hunt for 'Red Anna'
6. The Execution of Celebrity

The Contessa Munroe Mysteries (Cozy Mystery)

1. Corpse Reviver
2. Frostbite
3. Cobra's Fang

The Patrick Smythe Series (Crime)

1. The Disappearance of Russell Hadleigh
2. The Graves of Calgary Bay
3. The Fairy Pools Gathering

Austerley & Kirkgordon Series (Fantasy)

1. Crescendo!
2. The Darkness at Dillingham
3. Dagon's Revenge
4. Ship of Doom

Supernatural and Elder Threat Assessment Agency (SETAA) Series (Fantasy)

1. Scarlett O'Meara: Beastmaster

Island Adventures Series (Cosy Fantasy Adventure)

1. Surface Tensions

Dark Wen Series (Horror Fantasy)

1. The Blasphemous Welcome
2. The Demon's Chalice

Chapter 1

The runway light glared at him, cutting through the darkness outside. The white lights were brighter than the blue taxiway lights, informing the plane above exactly where to land. Although inside the visual control tower, it felt as if the elements were breaking in, for the wind that whipped along the runway—thankfully, straight down the nose of the aircraft—was also whipping around the tower, reaching some ten to fifteen metres high. The sliding door at the rear had never fully shut, and he could feel the slight draught coming in around his legs from outside.

He spun around in his seat and tapped into his weather console, changing the broadcast message to the aircraft, for there was now heavy hail in progress. He backed this up with a verbal message over the radiotelephony system, making sure the aircraft did not have to tune into the automated system.

Still, there was only one more to come. This aircraft in, back out, and off home he would go. Usually, he would sit with an assistant, but not today, for one assistant had reported in ill, meaning that the other assistant had to cover across two shifts. It wasn't a necessity, especially at this late hour when things were quiet, and so Eppy had to report the weather himself.

It wasn't like they weren't trained for it; it was just that they didn't do it very often, not with the assistant there.

'Localizer established,' came the pilot's voice across the RT.

'Continue approach,' said Eppy and looked down at the runway where a small vehicle with flashing lights was driving up and down.

'It's not settling,' came the call from the vehicle.

He never used the correct RT, did he? Never spoke properly on the radio. Maybe somebody should do something about it, thought Eppy, *but who would?* The old fireman had been there as long as anyone could remember but at least he knew what he was doing.

'So, what's the official report?'

'Eh, I think we're just going to have to say, wet, wet, wet.'

The runway, when being reported for contamination, was divided into three sections, and it was Aerodrome Operations' responsibility to inform the tower of the condition of the runway. At Mull, this was delegated to the fire service.

'Ops 1, Tower. Are you sure? There's no ice holding at all, is there?'

'Tower, there's a little bit here and there. It's just-—well, yes, there is some.'

'Ops1, roger. Let's go to weather standby, then.'

Eppy wasn't going to get caught out having ice mentioned on his runway and not preparing for the plane landing by having his fire crew at standby. It would probably be okay, and when he informed the aircraft of the runway state, they said they were happy to continue their approach. He sat back, looking out at the hail again, which had now lightened to such a degree that it caused him to have to correct the weather report again.

Eppy had been there for several years, and, in truth, he was quite settled into the job. There had been changes over the last few years, though. The runway had gone from grass to tarmac, and the taxiways had been upgraded. This was to allow them to take larger aircraft in, a boon for the island, and they had planes coming in from as far away as East Midlands and even Cardiff, not that they came very often.

There were maybe three large commercials a day, another two smaller ones, as well as some mail flights that were now routing their way. It meant that the airport had got somewhat busier. There was a steady stream of puddle jumpers in the summer, as he liked to refer to them—small aircraft flying over from Oban or down from Inverness. He also got trippers up from the south, and, in truth, the job was becoming more interesting because of it.

Sure, they weren't like these airfields further north, such as Stornoway or Wick which received the ferry flights, planes that were being brought over from other countries, usually by a transatlantic routing. Up there, they got some weird planes coming in, and some callers they knew from that region. They would send photographs down or post them up on social media, making Eppy slightly envious. On the other hand, they had to deal with all the customs, and Eppy was all for a quiet, if safe, life.

The money that had come in had really helped the airport, and Eppy finally felt he was working somewhere proper. He'd gone through all his training so many years back, thought he would be posted somewhere like Heathrow, Gatwick, or maybe even the terminal centres, but he found it hard to fit in and through various jobs, he'd ventured north to eventually settle on Mull.

The lifestyle was laid back, which suited him, and certainly the controlling wasn't as complex as other stations he'd worked at, but again, that didn't matter as long there was something to keep him going. The pay was good, especially for what they did. It wasn't as if it was expensive on Mull. Once upon a time, you'd have had to get the ferry to go off island, but not now. You could even get a commercial flight to here, there, or wherever, to connect up if you wanted to go abroad. Not that Eppy ever did.

He stared out at the runway again and saw that the hail had finished, but the temperature in front of him had just turned into a minus figure.

'Ops 1, Tower; is there any more ice for me?'

'There's a little bit, maybe one millimetre thick. I'd say it's covering about, what, twenty percent of the runway.'

'Ops 1, I'll put it to them. Well, we probably should de-ice after this.'

'Okay Tower. I'll tell the guys to get ready, but as we're on the weather standby, it's going to take time.'

'That's understood.'

The last flight in was not a large aircraft, but a Twin Otter that made its way from Inverness down to Mull and back once a day. It was really the brainchild of a businessman who lived in Mull but whose factory was in Inverness. The flight would go back and forward, last thing at night, but Eppy knew that the man often liked to disappear last thing at night, spend a night in a hotel before going to his work. He told him as much when Eppy had spoken to him in the terminal once, and he gave him a wink of an eye. Maybe the man had someone stashed away somewhere, some hot little number. *That would be nice,* thought Eppy. *Flying away to that every night, or at least a few nights a week.*

4

Eppy heard something downstairs, like a locker being closed, something being opened, but he shook his head. There was enough noise rattling around with the wind. It could be anything. It got funny at night, funny here on your own, last flight coming in. It was all right for the fire crew as the last flight only required four firefighters. Three of them were now out in the fire engine, one of two which were stationed at Mull and the Fire Chief, the last of the crew of four, was out on the runway in the Operation's vehicle. They always had somebody around them when they were waiting for flights if they were stuck in the station, someone to talk to.

Eppy had a TV in the tower because there were times they would sit there for maybe an hour with nothing happening, especially if it was through the night or during a late finish. Several of the controllers liked the TV on low to keep them interested and to keep the mind ticking over. Nothing worse than to actually fall asleep with a plane coming in, but it was not for Eppy. He preferred either to read his book, or just contemplate things. He was a thinker. Often, he would put the world to rights in his head while he stared out with the lights of the runway.

Eppy sat back in his chair, took a look out to his left, where he could see the lights of the plane approaching. One down, back out again, and it would be home time.

* * *

The Fire Chief spun off the runway, taking up position at the holding point on the far side of the runway from the terminal. 'Ops 1 is vacated,' he said loudly. There was no response. He gave a tut, picked up the handset again. 'Ops 1 has vacated the runway. We are clear of the runway.'

Still there was nothing. 'Ops 1, tower?'

The Fire Chief looked up at the tower and could see a figure in the control seat right where it should be. *Blasted radios*, he thought. *They keep saying it's blind spots here. It's not. It's just these bloody radios. They never fix them properly.*

'Tower, this is Ops 1. I have vacated the runway. Over.'

That would annoy him. OVER. Weren't allowed to say over. That would really annoy him. The Fire Chief smiled and looked along the runway where he could see the plane approaching.

'Carbon 4X Delta, final.'

They should call back to him, thought the Fire Chief. The ground radios were on their own circuit, separate to the air radio and it took the tower to connect the two. The Fire Chief wasn't worried when he then went to speak.

'Fire 1, this is Ops 1. Are you getting me?'

'Ops 1, this is Fire 1. You are loud and clear. Fives.'

'Roger.'

'Mull Tower, this is Carbon 4X Delta. We are now three-mile final. Confirm clear to land.'

There was silence on the radio and the Fire Chief watched the plane intently as it approached. There was nothing on the runway. He could land. That wasn't a problem, but the aircraft wouldn't unless it had been cleared to do so.

'Mull Tower, this is Carbon 4X Delta. Do you read me? Am I cleared to land?'

Again, there was silence, and the Fire Chief grabbed his binoculars and peered up at the tower. He was there. Eppy was there, but were his eyes closed? He hadn't fallen asleep, surely. *Bloody hell*, thought the Fire Chief. *What was this?*

'Carbon 4X Delta, we are now on our two-mile final.

6

Request permission to land. I say again, we request permission to land.'

Again, there was nothing. The Fire Chief was stuck because he couldn't enter the runway and cross over to the tower, having vacated it, without the tower's permission. The plane was less than two miles out now and at the end of the day, if it landed, he didn't want to be on the runway.

'Ops 1, Fire 1, what's going on?'

'Fire 1, Ops 1, keep the coms quiet. They're trying to land.'

'Roger.'

'Carbon X4X Delta, we are now one and a half-mile final. We need clearance to land. I say again, are we clear to land?'

Again, there was only silence. 'Carbon X4X Delta to anyone out there. Can you hear me?'

There was more silence. The Fire Chief watched the aircraft approach. It was now less than a mile out. *It shouldn't come below 400 feet*, he thought. He remembered that from his training.

The Fire Chief, in addition to being the Fire Chief, also came out during the night, operating in a role known as a Flight Information Service Officer and was capable of landing single aircraft without conflictions. He didn't do it that often, but he had to keep up his hours to maintain his licence. Usually, it was for medical emergencies, Helimed helicopters, or fixed-wing ambulance aircraft, Beech King Airs. He knew the basics of air traffic control, or at least to the level he'd attained.

'Carbon 4X Delta, we are going around. I say again, we are going around, and we'll take up a holding pattern.'

Ops 1 watched the aircraft climb and waited until it had gone past him above the runway.

'Ops 1, Fire 1, I'm going to go across to the tower, follow me on the taxiway.'

'Fire 1, Ops 1, Roger.'

'Ops 1 to all stations, I am now entering runway 23, and crossing to the tower. The Fire Chief put his foot down, took the operations vehicle across, and parked it at the base of the tower announcing he'd vacated to that location. As he stepped out, he saw the fire truck pulling up alongside him. Three of his charges jumped out.

'What's up?' asked the young driver.

'Let's not spook him by all going up,' said the Fire Chief. 'Just stay here, I'll give you a shout if I need you. I think he's just fallen asleep.' The others laughed. 'It's not a funny matter. He's cost that plane money.'

The Fire Chief entered the building, climbed up one flight of stairs and up the round circular staircase that led to the visual control room where the controllers worked. As he clanked up the metal staircase, he shouted up.

'Eppy. You there? Wake up, man. What are you doing?'

As the Fire Chief reached the top of the stairs, he saw Eppy in the chair, his head was pointing straight ahead but he was in a slightly reclined position. The Fire Chief walked over, putting his right hand on Eppy's left shoulder and began shaking him.

'Wake up. Bloody hell, we got a plane in the air here. Come on.' The Fire Chief started and stumbled back several paces as Eppy's head tipped forward, and then hung loosely.

'Eppy, are you all right? Are you there?'

The Fire Chief took hold of his radio. 'Fire 1, Fire Chief, get the three of you up here with the first aid kit now.'

The Fire Chief looked at Eppy's front and there was blood all down his clothing. He tried to lift the head to slap Eppy and see if he would wake up. As he did so, he noticed the long cut across the neck. It was why the head tipped forward and just sat there. The Fire Chief stepped backwards several times and then fell. He looked up at Eppy from the floor. There was a clanging on the staircase and the three charges ran up.

'What's the matter? What's up?'

'It's Eppy. He's dead. Somebody's cut his throat.'

Chapter 2

'Urquhart, are you ready to go yet?' asked Macleod, sticking his head out of his own office and glowering at his sergeant.

'Mull. It's Mull, we're going to be away for a while. I walk in here this morning and you tell me I'm going to Mull. Seoras, you've got to give me a chance to get my stuff together.'

'We've got a ferry to catch, and we don't all drive like you.'

'What is that meant to mean? I'll have you know I haven't had a speeding ticket in all my years of driving. Can you say that?'

Macleod backed down because Clarissa knew the answer.

Detective Inspector Macleod had arrived for work that morning at the Inverness Police Station, believing he was in for a quiet day. However, on arrival, a case was put to him, one of potential murder on the Isle of Mull. It wasn't the first time he had travelled away, as their patch may have been based in Inverness, but it reached to all corners of the highlands. The areas in Scotland he didn't cover, roughly, took a line from just above Glasgow and Edinburgh and then further south into the Borders. Anywhere else was up for grabs, depending on how busy other murder investigation teams were.

On hearing of the case, Macleod had called his team together, starting with Detective Sergeant Hope McGrath, his number two, who was on the way in from her home. She'd managed to spin the car and grab a case before coming back to the office.

Detective Constable Ross had been in at least thirty minutes before Macleod arrived, but he always carried a case in his car, which was just typical of the man. He was always prepared, always smart-looking. He was Macleod's computer expert and the engine room of the team. Macleod liked to think that he was the man pulling all the strings, but Ross was the one that made things happen. Any loose ends were tied up by Ross, any request for assistance and help completed by Ross.

Detective Sergeant Clarissa Urquhart was something else. When Macleod thought of his team, with Ross as the engine room, Hope McGrath his loyal captain, he sometimes wondered where to put Clarissa. It might be unkind to say she was his Rottweiler, but she came from an era when it was tough for women, even tougher than it was now. She grew up in an era when they were expected to be in the typing pool, and yet she never had been. She was also incredibly eccentric, dressed as if she was on the *Antiques Roadshow* and took no lip from anyone.

As much as she was coarse at times, Macleod liked her because he understood her. At the heart of Clarissa was a desire to get the job done, to see justice enacted, even if sometimes they needed a helping push. Hope McGrath, on the other hand was much more professional. Younger than Macleod by at least twenty years, he hoped that one day she'd take over from him. Yet while she was thorough, she didn't have that way of seeing the world that Macleod did, and he'd long given up the idea that she would. A fine detective in her own right, she'd have to run her own course, which was only right and proper.

Ross had reiterated the timetable for getting down to Oban and then across to Mull. As Hope had arrived and was ready, she said she would go down with Ross and set things up. Macleod had been waiting for his own baggage to arrive from home, and when it did, Ross and Hope had already set off, as Clarissa advised that she would bring the inspector down.

Macleod's door nearly shook off its hinges as Clarissa thundered a hand into the panels.

'Come in,' said Macleod, 'or simply just kick the thing off its hinges.'

The door swung open, and Clarissa stood with a shawl wrapped around her, an attractive brooch pinning it tight. Today her hair was purple, and she wore a face that said she had got out of bed far too early. She was wearing tartan trousers underneath, and Macleod, never a connoisseur of fashion, simply shook his head.

'Don't even start. Black trousers, black tie, black jacket, white shirt. You always look like you're going to a funeral.'

Again, Macleod, couldn't retaliate. He'd grown up on the Isle of Lewis, where everyone seemed to have a black suit and tie. Funerals were a way of life out there and if someone died in the village, everyone went. Sometimes Macleod wondered how any work got done on the island.

'Anyway, your carriage awaits, my lord.'

'Just stick to the speed limit,' said Macleod.

'As I said, I have never been done for speeding, unlike some people.'

You looked that up, Macleod thought to himself. *You actually went into the records to find that out. It was not my fault. I didn't know the speed limit. Well, actually, it was my fault.'* He turned and grabbed his bag from behind his desk, and slung it over his shoulder along with a suit bag.

'What colour is the suit in the bag?' asked Clarissa. Macleod looked up at her. 'No, don't give me that clear-off-Clarissa look, just tell me what colour is it?'

'Black.'

'Why don't you bring a different colour suit? Why don't you have several suits? I can pick some out for you.'

'Jane can pick them out for me. If I got you to get me a suit, it'd be bright blue, or that yellow colour.'

Clarissa looked with fierce eyes at Macleod. 'There's no need to be like that. Yellow isn't your colour, maybe something a bit more beige.' She hung the comment out there for Macleod to snap, but he was no fish in the pond; he wouldn't take the bait.

'Car, now,' said Macleod. 'Let's get down there so we don't miss this ferry.'

'We won't miss the ferry. We'll be there.' With that, Clarissa turned, walked into the outer office and grabbed her own bag, but didn't wait for Macleod. When he got to the car park, she was sitting in her sporty green number. The car had only two seats in the front and some boot space behind.

'You're not putting the hood up?'

'No, I'm not,' said Clarissa. I'm keeping it down. 'It's fresh air today since it's lovely.'

Macleod wrapped his coat up around him. As he placed his baggage in the boot, he reached inside one of his bags, and took out a hat, pulling it over his head.

'The black beanie goes well with the suit, sir,' said Clarissa, smiling.

'Don't you sir me. Let's go and remind me to have a go at Hope and Ross.'

'What for?' asked Clarissa.

'Abandoning me with some wild woman.' He didn't smile. There was no way he was letting her see him smile.

* * *

The journey down had been a long one. By the time they arrived at the airport, it was late in the afternoon and no flights had come in that day for the air traffic control tower was closed. As Macleod walked towards it, he could see the white van of the forensic unit and Jona Nakamura detailing her team.

'Where do we start, Hope?' asked Macleod.

'I spoke to Jona, and she wants more time up there. The victim died, sitting up in his seat in the control tower. They had an aircraft coming in, which then went around.'

'Which then did what?'

'It went around,' said Hope. 'It's like it couldn't land. It wasn't given permission, so it took off and went up into the hold above. The Fire Chief then managed to relay information to it and talked to the Scottish Centre, who diverted it elsewhere. I think it went back to Inverness.

'Was the plane in anyway involved?' asked Macleod.

'No,' said Hope. 'I don't see how.'

Macleod looked around him and saw the wide-open space of the airfield. There was a terminal building in one corner, small, but not unreasonable, considering the size of the island.

'Was that place open?' asked Macleod.

'Yes, Seoras. The terminal was open, but you don't get to come this side. They have a small number of security to stop you. We'll be checking up obviously, but we don't have any reports of anyone being the wrong side.'

'There's not really a high fence around the airfield, is there though?'

'No,' said Hope.

The grass that was beside the runway and taxiways had been cleared but the grass that lay beyond the runways and the taxiways looked wild. The perimeter fence resembled something that would be seen in a farmer's field which could be jumped over quite easily.

'It's not really designed to keep people out, Seoras,' said Hope. 'Designed to keep out sheep, or animals.'

'What you're saying is anybody could come onto the airfield quite easily.'

'Well, there are signs. *This is an airfield; keep off.*'

'Most killers don't stop for signs. If they did, we would put them everywhere.'

'True,' said Hope. 'Make the job a whole lot easier. Last night, I've been told, there were four firefighters on.'

'Why?' asked Macleod.

'Because you need them, Seoras. Normally there's six but you need to have at least four for the type of plane that was landing. Everyone else had gone home except for John Epson, known as Eppy, the dead man. He was in the tower working the plane coming in and out, his assistant having left some time before. Apparently, one of them went sick yesterday, so while he would normally have an assistant in with him, he didn't yesterday.

'When did they leave?' asked Macleod.

'At least two hours before that last plane came in. Obviously, we'll be doing interviews with them.'

'The four firemen. What about them?'

'They're gathered over in the fire station at the moment. We can go and have a word if you wish. The Fire Chief's there amongst them. He was one of them, an Ian Morrison. They are not in a good way. I imagine it's quite a tight knit little group here.'

'How do you mean?'

'Well, you see the big airports, and you wonder how much the air traffic get to mix with the fire crews and—I mean, you look at Edinburgh's tower, it's massive. They are all the way up there. Here the fire crew could pop in and out of the tower. The fire crew did several different jobs as well. It sounds very different to the big operation.

'Somebody didn't get on well with him,' said Macleod, pushing his tie up. 'Let's go over to the fire service and see what these four that were on last night can tell us.'

As Macleod strode across, a rather rotund man started waving at them.

'Who is that?' asked Macleod.

'I believe that's the airport manager, Curtis James.' The man was huffing and puffing as he ran across. 'Inspector. Inspector.'

Macleod watched the man arrive. He stopped, gulping in air before rising up, trying to make himself attain his full height. Macleod saw the man's eye catch a look at Hope and he saw it linger.

'You are Mr James, I hear,' said Macleod.

'Curtis James,' said the man, puffing hard again. 'I'm the airport manager. When can we open?'

'I'm sorry?'

'When can we open?'

'Well, you still have a dead body up in that tower,' said

Macleod. 'I'm running a murder investigation and I need to interview all your staff and I'll need to speak to you as well. I'm just going over to talk to the fire section, but I'll be getting around to you very soon, sir, and we can talk properly about how this murder investigation is going to run.'

'Perhaps I could speak to your assistant,' said Curtis as his eyes roved up and down over Hope.

'Assistant?' said Macleod. 'She's not my assistant. That is Detective Sergeant Hope McGrath. She's required to be with me to interview your fire service. We'll be seeing you in the very near future, sir. I suggest you go back to your office and wait for us to arrive. You won't be opening today; I'll tell you that.'

The man drew in a deep breath. 'We need to open soon. It's all money. All money.'

'There's a man dead up there,' said Macleod. 'You could show a little bit of compassion.' *Instead of eyeing up my sergeant,* thought Macleod.

'I'm well aware I've got a dead man up there,' said the airport manager. 'It's going to play hell with the rosters. Do you know how long it takes to train these people?'

Macleod's nostrils flared but Hope stepped across in front of him. 'Mr James, back to your office now, please.' The man smiled at her, turned slowly before looking back at her. 'I wouldn't rush,' said Hope. 'The journey over here seems to have tired you out.'

Macleod almost burst out laughing. Sometimes he went to defend Hope, especially when he saw somebody being lecherous around her or someone trying to take advantage. He should know better for she was more than capable of defending herself. That being said, Macleod was itching to let Clarissa

17

go and interview the airport manager, for she'd tear him to shreds.

Once inside the fire station, Macleod and Hope were led through to a small canteen area where a number of firefighters were sitting around. 'There's more than four here,' said Macleod. 'Can I speak to who's in charge?'

An older man stood up, slightly greying in the hair, but Macleod noticed he looked strong. 'I'm Ian Morrison, the Fire Chief, officer.'

'Sorry,' said Macleod. 'I should've introduced myself. Detective Inspector Seoras Macleod. This is Detective Sergeant Hope McGrath. Were all of you on last night?'

'No,' said Ian. 'Just me, and three others from the team. Two of the boys and then Margaret there. She's nearly been at this job as long as me. Looks better though. Hasn't aged her the way it's aged me.'

Macleod could see the dry humour being forced out. Underneath, he could tell the man was unsettled and no wonder.

'I heard you found the body, sir,' said Macleod.

'That's right. The four of us were out on the airfield. You see, the aircraft was coming in and there was hail and possible ice on the runway, so Eppy called the weather standby. That means we took one of the fire trucks, we sat down at the holding point—that's the place where you go on to the runway—and we waited in case anything happened.'

'Such as what?' asked Macleod.

'Well, if the aircraft hit ice then slid off the runway; it just means we're closer. It's risk management.'

'The four of you were in the fire vehicle?' said Macleod.

'No,' said Ian. 'I was in the operation's vehicle checking the runway. I was out there the whole time.'

'Can you confirm then he was still alive while you were out there?'

'Well, he spoke,' said Ian. 'I assumed it was him.'

'Inspector,' said Hope, 'the airfield has tapes. Everything that's said over the radio is recorded. This is demanded by the CAA, the Civil Aviation Authority. The playback of the tapes, that'll confirm what the Fire Chief is saying.'

'The four of you were out there and not upstairs. On that basis, it seems like you four have got good alibis.' Macleod took Hope to one side. 'We want those recordings for the last words and to see if there's anything on those tapes. We also want CCTV. They've got to have CCTV around here.'

'I imagine Ross is already on it but I'll check up. We'll get onto interviewing everybody here as well,' said Hope.

'Probably best we go and speak to the airport manager before he has a hernia. I was hoping this was going to be easy,' said Macleod. 'If those four were out there and somebody came in from outside, we need to establish what went on here yesterday. Who was where and when? Also, who's got the opportunity to go in? When Jona's done, I want to get a look at that tower.'

'Of course, Inspector,' said Hope, keeping it formal as there were plenty of ears around. Then she leaned forward and whispered to Macleod. 'Guess we better go and see my admirer then.'

Chapter 3

The airport manager's office was at the terminal building, which was known as being on landside. Macleod was having to quickly come to terms with the nomenclature regarding the airfield. When the airport was opened, airside was meant to be off-limits unless air traffic control were talking to you. If you wanted to move about on the taxiways, the runway, or indeed some of the other paths around the airfield, you'd have to speak to air traffic. The aprons where the aircraft parked at the terminal building was also known as the Airside, but here people could operate freely if they had the correct jurisdiction.

The main question for Macleod, namely, if there could be people there at the time of the arrival, was yes, but it was unlikely due to the inclement weather, and the fact that the Fire Chief in the operation vehicle would be the person marshalling the aircraft. The ground crew of the airline company would only be there once the aircraft was close to landing.

Macleod entered the terminal building and spotted the manager's office. He made a beeline for it but was abruptly stopped by someone in a blue security uniform.

'Excuse me, sir. Where do you think you're going?'

'I'm going to the airport manager,' said Macleod.

'You can't do that. I'm afraid he's a busy man.'

Hope stepped in front of Macleod seeing he was starting to seethe.

'Excuse me, I'm Detective Sergeant Hope McGrath. We're going in to see the airport manager. This is Detective Inspector Seoras Macleod and we're here investigating the death of your colleague.'

'Okay, but the rules are that you don't go in and see the airport manager without an appointment.'

'Really?' said Macleod. 'That's where I'm going. I'll go where I want.'

'No, you don't, sir. You need to stay in the terminal building. Those are the rules.'

'This is a police investigation,' said Macleod. 'Kindly step aside.'

Hope turned to Macleod, putting her hands up in front of the man and blocking the security guard.

'Why don't you run on and see the airport manager, sir, while I have a word with our friend?'

'I think that's a good idea, McGrath. Kindly explain to him where his jurisdiction lies in all of this.' Macleod stormed off and Hope was left with a rather bemused young man simply trying to do his job.

'It's a police investigation. We'll go where we want, when we want,' said Hope.

'I understand if it's a safety issue. We'll tell people what we're doing, but we are to be facilitated at all times. Did your security training never tell you any of this?'

'It's just we're not allowed to let anybody in there. I'm not going to let anybody see the airport manager.'

'He'll see us,' said Hope 'because if he doesn't talk to us here, he'll talk to us down at the local station. He probably doesn't want that. I suspect he's trying to stop the press and anybody else coming in to see him.'

'Yes,' said the man. 'You don't have any badges or anything?'

Hope pulled out her ID and held it up in front of the man. 'I'm going to see your airport manager and join my boss. I suggest in the future, you make sure you understand what his face looks like and mine. He won't take kindly to this interruption again.'

'That's understood,' said the man, shaking a little. 'It's just I was told.'

'I know,' said Hope. 'You were told. Now, I've told you correctly.'

In some ways, Hope felt sorry for the man, just doing his job, and probably told he had more authority than he really had. She was all for making sure that everything operated safely on an airfield, but at the moment it was closed. No planes could come in or depart. She didn't really see what the big issue was.

Hope knocked on the door of the airport manager's office. It was very quiet but she heard a 'Come in,' and closed the door behind her. She saw Curtis James, sitting rather gloomily behind his desk, frowning at Macleod. As she entered, she saw the man looked up and smile broadly.

'I don't need to detain you, Inspector,' said James. 'I can easily go through any questions you have with your sergeant.'

'You'll go through the questions with me because I think I may need to put a few ground rules down about what's going on here, Mr James,' said Macleod. 'First off, this airport is closed until I say it's opened. I don't care what else is happening.'

'We've got an inspection coming up, one we have to get through or else we would be closed permanently.'

'You've got a dead body up in the tower,' said Macleod. 'Would you kindly point out what's more important than that? It indicates you've got a killer on your airfield.'

'Not necessarily.'

'How would that work?' asked Macleod.

'It could have been a suicide.'

Macleod rolled his eyes, looked over at Hope as if somewhere there were cameras watching them, and they were soon to appear on a comedic television program.

'I think, Mr James, what the Inspector feels is most suicides don't tend to slit their own throats, and then manage to hide the knife before quietly dying.'

Curtis James nodded, in a way that made Hope think he may not have fully understood what she was saying.

'One thing we can't have, Inspector, is the press around here.'

'What are you going to do?' asked Macleod. 'Kick them off the island? Send them all back over on the ferry? You've just had a murder. Of course, there's going to be press here. They'll be kept away from all the important areas while we do our work. Trust me, I know how to handle the press. As for you and your staff, unless you're talking to us, you'll have to deal with them the same as anybody else. Enough about you and your airfield, Mr James. I want to know about John Epson. Who was he?'

'John had been here for a while,' said Curtis. 'Quite a quiet man, as well. As far as I understand, nobody here would want to hurt him. He came in, got on with his job. You never heard an angry word between him or anybody else. He was very competent at it; knew what he was doing. Some people say he was overqualified. He could have worked further south, some of the big airfields, maybe even the big centres. I've got no history of trouble with him on our records even before I arrived. Every report is fine. He wasn't too keen to get involved in any new projects; if I'm honest, he tried to give me a wide berth.'

Macleod saw Hope smirk, and then forgave her because he was thinking that he would give the manager a wide berth if he worked here as well.

'In truth, the boys on the airside would understand him better than I did. Over here, I deal only with security, passengers. Air traffic kind of takes care of itself—fire service as well.

'Aren't you responsible for the airfield, though?' asked Hope. 'As I understand it, the aerodrome authority has overall charge, required to look after the taxiways, the runway, make sure everything's up to standard, lights and that.'

'That's correct; that is my job.'

'Well, then you'll have been talking to people working on that side.'

'To be honest, it's just people at head office that take care of that. I just sign most things off.'

McGrath stared at the man, trying to size him up. She looked around the office and saw a simple calculation written on a whiteboard, something to do with VAT.

'Well, Mr James, I think we're going to talk with your fire crew again. Confirm he didn't have any enemies. We'll also be pulling in air traffic, finding out about his colleagues. I'll send Ross over to speak with you to make appointments. Be warned though, no mucking about. If you do, he'll tell me. Our priority here is to find the killer, Mr James. The airfield

24

stays shut as long as I need that to be the case. If I don't, I'll happily let you open it.' Macleod stood up and walked out of the room, followed by Hope. When the door closed, Macleod looked over to her.

'What do you make of him?'

'He does like the women, doesn't he?' said Hope; 'the whole time hardly looking at you, always looking at me. Not my face, either.'

'I hate to break it to you,' said Macleod. 'I don't think it was just you, either. I think he would look at any woman.'

'You don't have to enlighten me on a man like that,' said Hope. 'One thing though, when he said he just signs everything off, I think he was telling the truth. Did you see the calculation on the whiteboard?'

'VAT. Not the most difficult, is it?' said Macleod.

'No, still doesn't rule him out. He seems to be somebody who likes to get his own way, trying to tell you when he was going to open the airport,' chuckled Hope.

'Indeed,' said Macleod. 'Back to the fire section. I want to talk with them again, especially the four who were on. It clearly can't have been them, but they may have good insights and we know they have nothing to hide. Tell Ross to get the rest of the staff lined up for interviews, take advantage of the place being closed.'

Macleod walked outside. After dragging security down to open up a gate for him to go airside, he strode to the fire station, accompanied by Hope, to the office of the Fire Chief, Ian Morrison.

'I told you last time, Inspector,' said Morrison, 'the four of us were on weather standby. We couldn't get anywhere near the tower. Couldn't even suggest who did it?'

'I'm not here because I think you did it,' said Macleod. 'I'm here because I need to know about what went on in this airfield. I've spoken to your airport manager and frankly, I'm not sure he knows that much about what goes on here.'

'No pulling the wool over your eyes then,' said Morrison. 'It's quite a tight-knit community in some ways because we're a small airfield. We do all the marshalling, we do all the sweeping, the grass cutting, and the runway de-icing. We marshal the aircraft in, we see everyone that works on the airplane, we see the air traffic control tower because we talk to them constantly. They come over here during breaks sometimes, and we pop up there. It works well. Sometimes we get unusual aircraft that we don't have the steps for. We have to use different devices to get people down from specific aircraft. It's good to be on top of things. Good when everybody knows what's going on.'

'Do you know of anyone with anything against Mr Epson?'

'Amongst the controllers, no. I know my own crew. Some people don't get on with certain other people, but not to the detriment of the job. They know what's expected, they do it. Yes, you hear this rumour, that rumour, whatever, but you know what? You don't get overworked up here. It's not a big airfield. It's a nice number, do what you need to do. Make sure you're covered, and just look after what goes on.'

As Macleod was speaking with Morrison, there came a knock at the door. Hope and Macleod turned to see one of the firefighters, tears streaming down her face. Emerson jumped up at the sight and raced to the woman.

'You were on that night,' said Hope, recognising the woman from earlier on.

'This is Margaret, Margaret Humble, been here nearly as

long as me. What's up, Margaret? Are you okay?'

'John,' she said, almost oblivious to the police officers standing about her. 'He's dead; he's really gone.'

Morrison took the woman and guided her into the seat he'd vacated, before asking Hope to keep an eye on her. The Fire Chief stepped outside and shouted to one of the other firefighters to bring in a cup of tea. As an afterthought, he asked Macleod and Hope if they wanted any, before returning and going down on one knee beside Margaret Humble. The woman was clearly distraught. Morrison knelt, assessing her, and gave her the cup of tea.

'Did you know John Epson well?' asked Macleod. The woman burst into tears.

'I think it's delayed shock, Inspector,' said Morrison. 'I was wanting her to go home and somebody to go with her, to make sure she's okay. She's not fit to be in here and with no planes coming. I know you want to talk to everyone, but maybe it's best if Margaret makes her way home. I'll get somebody, one of the boys to run her home.'

'I think that's a very wise move, Mr Morrison, but I'll tell you what, McGrath here will give her a lift. We do need to speak to Miss Humble, but maybe a setting away from here would be better for her. I'm sure everything's quite fresh in her mind.'

'I can do that, boss,' said Hope. She went to leave but Macleod grabbed her.

'That looks like more than shock to me,' he whispered to Hope. 'See if you can find what's going on.'

'Well, maybe you're right, but it was pretty nasty up there and she got a view of it.'

'I know,' said Macleod, 'but call it my instinct. She looks

distressed on a deeper level than that.'

Macleod watched Hope help the woman outside the airfield and into Hope's car. Macleod realised that he'd probably have to disappear back to his lodgings later in Clarissa's green car.

Margaret Humble needed help, as Macleod watched Hope place her in the car. He couldn't help but get the feeling that the woman was grieving in a deeper fashion than anyone else around here.

As he stood watching with Morrison, he asked, 'Did she know Epson well?'

'Not sure if she knew him any better than anybody else. Sat up there, we're down here, and, yes, we say hello. I don't think there's anything more to it.'

Macleod nodded and was about to make his way back inside the fire station to talk to the rest of the firefighters when he felt his phone vibrate.

'If you'll excuse me for a moment, Mr Morrison,' said Macleod. He retrieved his mobile from his pocket and pressed the text message button at the bottom. It was from Hope. It was a simple but revealing message. *Margaret says she's his lover. Will take her home; find out more.*

Chapter 4

As Hope pulled the car into the small driveway, she looked at the tiny cottage with a smart lawn around it. Little flowerbeds were packed tightly in around it, and she thought in a better day, the place would look magnificent. The cottage was old-looking, sure, a little run down, but it certainly had bags of character.

Before she could say anything, Margaret Hamble stepped out of the car and was walking along the short path to the front door. As Hope got out of the car to follow, the woman turned, waving at Hope, encouraging her to come along as well. Margaret Hamble was only about five feet five, and Hope, at six feet, seemed to dwarf the woman. As Hope reached the front door, still swinging open from Margaret having walked through, she closed it behind her, but not before taking a quick look up and down the road, just in case any of the newspaper boys were about. It was quite remote at Mull, so maybe they'd be easier to spot. Back on the mainland, they'd be all over you.

'I'll put a kettle on,' said Margaret. 'I take it you'll take tea?'

Hope wanted coffee, but she wasn't going to force the woman to do any entertaining. 'Tea is fine,' she said. 'It's a nice place you've got.'

'When you're on your own,' came the voice from the kitchen,

'you've time to do so much.'

Hope entered the kitchen and found it to be neatly laid out. There was an old Aga stove. This was contrasted by the modern digital radio sitting on the windows sill.

'All a bit of a mishmash, isn't it?'

'Do you live alone?' asked Hope.

Margaret stopped, staring at her. 'No. I guess that's what you want to know. Isn't it? If we had a falling out or anything.'

'I just want to know about your relationship,' said Hope. 'No one's saying you're suspect. No one's saying you did anything. In fact, you have an alibi for last night. So, it's really more to see if anyone might be jealous of the two of you.'

'Jealous?' queried Margaret as she filled the kettle. 'How could anyone be jealous? Nobody knew. John was a very upright man. He wanted everyone to know when we first started seeing each other, but I didn't. Tongues wag around here. It's not the sort of thing I need. Besides, then you get all the questions. When's he moving in? When are you getting together? When you're out in company, you have to be seen to be all over each other or something's wrong.

'We were both just older. Come to that point in life where we enjoyed each other's company. He'd come around here in the evening, that'd be about six, seven. I'd do a bit of supper, some nights we didn't say a word. We just sat and he'd be reading, I'd be reading in there in front of the fire. It was more a connection in some ways.'

'It wasn't a physical relationship?' said Hope.

'Oh, no, it was. I mean, I'm not dead. It might not be like you see on the telly, rampantly on the back of a chair and hey, here we go for the next weekend. Probably a lot more just holding each other rather than all that work out,' said, Margaret, almost laughing, 'but it's what we needed, the pair of us. I hope you can understand that.'

Hope thought about her man John, back in Inverness, and yes, she understood sometimes you just needed to be held. She did pray that the other side of the relationship didn't die off too quickly, either. 'Why are you sure that nobody else knew?'

'Because we kept it very discreet. You see, I'm a church deacon, and my Baptist church, that's up in Tobermory. We're a few miles out and I lost my husband just over two years ago. Eppy was strong, kind, caring, and I needed someone in my life. I had been with my husband since I was sixteen. Suddenly, there came this massive hole. Eppy wasn't then to replace him though, Eppy was just Eppy.

'When I said to him, I didn't want anybody to know, because I knew it was only what, a month after Tom passed on, and the church wouldn't have understood it. Some of the people at work wouldn't have understood it, either. I told him I didn't want anyone to know and then it became our little secret. Just us. There's something about that, something that ties the bonds closer to each other, because it's your secret because you have to be hidden. It's also quite exciting in some ways. Can you understand that bit?'

'Did you need the excitement? Was there another point when you thought, 'Do you know what, we should really tell people.''

'Well, Eppy kept saying that. I mean he was morally robust. Things should be above board, but he knew I wasn't ready. The trouble is that once you have gone quiet and secret, if you then reveal why or anything about it, people ask you why you didn't do that in the first place? It looks like you have something to hide.'

'Did you?' asked Hope.

'Yes, I did. Me. I wasn't ready to face anything else. A hard-enough time from people going on about how wonderful my husband was. He was good, but never as good as people made out. Nobody can live up to that.'

'You basically had what? An affair?'

'Only in the sense that it was secret. We weren't hurting anybody. It was just me and Eppy. Eppy was single, I was a widow. Seemed natural.'

'Did you not ever want to be able to stroll down the street together?' asked Hope.

'We did. We went abroad, quietly abroad into the sun. Sometimes we did some daft things, but you know what, it was good for me. Lifted me up from where I was.'

'Well, I'm truly sorry,' said Hope, 'that he passed on, but I'm going to need to ask you some questions. Some you might not be too keen on answering and they may hurt as well. So, I'm sorry for that in advance, but I need to ask.'

Margaret started pouring the tea, but she simply nodded.

'Well,' said Hope, 'can you think of anyone who could do this to Mr Epson?'

'You mean at the station or amongst the controllers?'

'Anyone.'

'No, Eppy was a man of character. There weren't many people that would argue with him. He didn't pick fights. The only person I heard fight with him was Julia Fluke.'

'Who's Julia Fluke?' asked Hope. 'I'm sorry, I just haven't gotten up to date with all the names yet.'

'Julia is one of the controllers,' said Margaret. 'Fairly recent, something about an old hand though, like John was. I was around at John's and suddenly there was a knock at the door, so I hid. We had a thing where we dropped our cars off a mile away and walked. In truth, this gave us an excuse to walk back half a mile with the other person. Hell, guess we really didn't need that, did we? Seems daft now, like a pair of teenagers just keeping away from their parents.'

'You were talking about Julia Fluke,' said Hope. 'Do you know what the row was about?'

'No, but it was intense, so I hid. I couldn't hear properly. They were two rooms away, but voices were raised. When I asked John about it, he just said, "Never mind". Didn't want to waste our time together with stuff like that. He could be a bit closed like that, in fairness. Didn't like to share the weight of the world. But for all that, I did love him. Wasn't just some wild fling; I wasn't just on the rebound. No, there was definitely love there and I think he did love me, too.'

'I hope you don't mind me saying but you seem a bit old to be a firefighter. Punching on the small side as well.'

Margaret looked up from her tea at Hope and smiled. 'We can't all be a giant like yourself. You must get some attention,' she said. 'Six-foot, red hair. You look the part, don't you?'

'Looking the part isn't what we're about though,' said Hope. 'It's about what's between the ears.'

'You probably have that as well. I'm not having a go,' said Margaret. 'I work-out at the station. This is what I do. It's not that stressful, keeps me fairly fit. The hours don't matter to me because I'm footloose and fancy-free. Even when Tom was here. He didn't bother. We had our life, a way of working. I don't have any kids. Then there's working for Ian and he's very helpful. You saw him today? He's good; he cares for his people. He comes from back in the day when there were hardly any planes landing and you wonder if anybody was actually sober

33

on the airfield.'

Margaret laughed. 'Back in the day some of the aircraft, you wonder if you should be sober going up in them.'

Then came a hysterical laugh from the woman. *Inappropriate*, Hope thought. Once she saw her bend over and start to cry, she knew the woman had tried to hide the pain but had failed miserably.

'Do you know who stood to gain from John's death?' asked Hope. 'I mean financially and that.'

'Don't know. I'm not sure he has anybody. I never saw a will or any solicitor's instructions.'

'Did he get on right with his fellow controllers?' asked Hope.

'Like I said, the only time I ever heard him argue is that time with Julia Fluke, but outside of that, he seemed happy with them. He was forever giving Curtis hassle.'

'Curtis James, the airport manager?'

'Yes. Man would come up with temporary instructions for this, temporary instructions for that. John used to say to me they don't even make sense on any level. Badly worded, badly written junk.'

'Do you think Mr James is not capable of doing his job?' asked Hope.

'Well, it depends what job you give him, doesn't it? Look, it's not up to me. They put him in; it's up to them how he runs the place. I just do my job and try to enjoy life.' The woman began to cry again.

'Have you got anybody about?' asked Hope. 'Anybody who can come in and sit with you?'

'Neighbours, two down. She'll come up. I'll be fine. Back in tomorrow. Life goes on, doesn't it?'

'No,' said Hope. 'Sometimes life comes to a grinding halt.

It's okay. You can come to a grinding halt with it. As long as you get started up again later. At least that's what I've been told.'

Hope thanked the woman, returned to her car where, as she sat down, her phone began to ring. It was Macleod.

'Do we know where we're staying yet, Hope?' asked Macleod, 'because frankly, I feel like getting off this airfield.'

'Why?'

'Basically, I'm just looking at my other Detective Sergeant and she's going full tilt at that Curtis James.'

'I could see how he could wind her up.'

'You don't have to wind her up. Anyway,' said Macleod, 'you better get back here because I might not have a Detective Sergeant for long. I might have to handcuff her when she punches somebody.'

Hope laughed. 'I'm making my way back now, Seoras. When I get back you can finish up and head back. We can get to work on the personnel files and CCTV through the night. I'm in the process of getting those interviews lined up for the morning.'

'It's a good idea,' said Macleod. As she closed down the call, Hope looked back at the cottage beside her. It wasn't often she came to a case where she saw people who weren't suspects, saw people distinctly removed from the case but distinctly hurt about what had happened. Sometimes you had to let yourself feel for people. Tonight, she was feeling for Margaret who had lost her husband two years ago and now she was losing her . . . lover? No, that was the wrong word. Companion. That was more how she described it, wasn't it? A companion.

Hope started the car and drove back to the airport realising that despite the cold air, it was at least dry. The previous night had been hailstorms passing through according to the weather reports. Certainly, something dark had come into the small community around the airport. Would they find it? Hope was sure of it. Between her and Macleod, they'd get to the bottom of this one.

Chapter 5

Clarissa Urquhart stood facing what was now a biting wind and bemoaned the lack of shelter. She was standing on the airfield, just a little way off the runway, monitoring the team. They were searching in the area, combing it to see if the murder weapon was left behind. So far, they had progressed from one side of the airfield, over the runway and were now searching the other side. Clarissa stood at the fire practice ground, where there was a burnt-out car, and a mock-up of an aircraft, with steps leading into it, but you could see fuel lines, presumably that fed the fire that would be set inside it.

Clarissa looked at the team she had gathered. There were some police officers, but there were also members of other emergency services. She had called the Coastguard in and the teams from Mull had gathered at the airfield, but because of the size of the job, others had come over from the mainland, arriving on the ferry. In some ways the search was painstaking, for they weren't looking for a quick sprint across the ground, rather a slow protracted rummage through the long grass.

Clarissa wasn't searching, but generally standing around the organisers of that search, ready to advise if anything found was critical or not. In terms of actually searching squares and different areas, she allowed the professionals to do their job. Part of her wanted to be inside the office buildings, where Macleod was. She was feeling too old to be standing out here, despite the rather large shawl around her.

Clarissa could see a car approach along the runway, lights flashing and recognised it as the operations vehicle. As it got closer, she tried to see who was in it and she thought she could see the Fire Chief at the driver's wheel. As the vehicle pulled into the fire practice ground, the man gave Clarissa a little wave, but she saw another person sitting beside him. Although she hadn't spoken to him, she quickly recognised the airport manager, Curtis James.

As he stepped out of the car, his shoulders all puffed up, she guessed his type. He stomped over before stopping in front of her and then, as if no one was there, ran his hands around the inside of his belt, pulling his trousers up and tucking his belly over the top.

'I'm Curtis James, the Airport Manager.'

'That's nice to know,' said Clarissa. 'Why are you here?'

'I was looking for Macleod. We spoke earlier, but I couldn't find him, so I've come to you as next in charge.'

'Then you've come to the wrong person,' said Clarissa, smugly. 'I'm actually not his deputy.'

'What? Who is?'

'Detective Sergeant McGrath,' said Clarissa. 'You'll be wanting her.'

'But she's a mere kid compared to yourself.'

Clarissa bit her lip. She remembered Macleod's word with her a month ago, where he explained that she needed to be a little bit more diplomatic when speaking to rude people.

38

Clarissa hadn't seen why, but the boss wanted it, so that's what she would do.

'I think you'll find that DS McGrath is actually of a legal age where she can take part in the job and run it. She is, in fact, no kid.'

'No,' said Curtis. 'But she's, I mean . . .'

'You mean what?' asked Clarissa.

'Well, I thought she was just . . .'

'The eye candy he likes on his arm, while he sends out me here to do the job because I'm professional and know what I'm about?'

'Yes,' said Curtis. 'No. No. That's . . .'

'I'll advise her when she gets back,' said Clarissa. 'I'm sure she'd like to be informed.'

'Where is Macleod?'

'I left him back in the building on the other side of the airfield. If you don't mind, I'm trying to run a search here. Currently, you've just come in, driven all over my airfield, and now pitched up and harassed me. I think the best thing you can do, sir, is to go back to your office and take a seat. I'm sure if the detective inspector wants you, he'll come for you.'

Clarissa turned her back on him, looking across at the searchers, not that she needed to, but merely to show her annoyance with the man. Her shawl was flung round again, not that it needed repositioning, but again, to make the man feel as if he was simply being brushed off her shoulder.

She heard the footsteps, then the tap on the shoulder. 'Now, look here, dear.'

Clarissa spun around. 'Dear? It's Detective Sergeant.'

'Well, I'm the Airport Manager and this is my airfield.'

'Well, it was until you let somebody die on it,' said Clarissa.

The talk with Macleod, it was starting to go out the window. 'At that point, because there's been a murder, it's actually our airfield and we'll dictate what happens. At the moment, Detective Inspector Macleod says that this airfield isn't open. I'm sure he told you that to your face. You can't bypass him like this, you cannot come to me and, God forbid, do not try and sweet talk Detective Sergeant McGrath, because if it's any way like the way you deal with me, your arse will end up behind bars.'

'I don't have to take that,' said the airport manager.

'No, you don't,' said Clarissa. 'You can get back in the car and get that rather decent Fire Chief to drop you off at your office and sit there. You will take it if you come at me with that attitude again. Detective Inspector Macleod has declared that this airport is closed. We are conducting investigations on the airfield.'

'Well, you need to hurry up.'

'No, we don't. We need to do a thorough job. We have got plenty of assistance here and people giving up their time and generally, being a positive influence for this community. I have no idea why you are here, but I suggest you leave.'

The man huffed, turned around and Clarissa could hear him berating the Fire Chief, telling him all the things that she'd said to him. She couldn't resist a look to see the Fire Chief's face and the bright smile across it.

Clarissa walked over to the search advisor, who started to explain where they would move to next, but she was aware that she hadn't heard the vehicle leave. Again, there were footsteps behind her, and she was anticipating the tap on the shoulder, but it didn't come.

'Excuse me. It is Detective?'

Clarissa turned around and saw the Fire Chief, Ian Morrison.
'It's Detective Sergeant Urquhart,' she said.

'I apologise for getting in your way, but it's his nibs back there, asked me to come up and basically, harass you again. I'm not going to do that. I'm just going to say thanks for what you're doing, and I'll go back and tell him I got nowhere as well.'

'Oh, you can stay,' said Clarissa, smiling at the man. 'It's going to be a while. We've searched most of the other side of the airfield, but we're combing this side and we may go back over it again. If we find something, there may even be longer delays. In truth, I don't see your airfield opening for at least a day or two, if not longer. How are you doing, anyway? You were the one that found him.'

'In truth,' said Morrison, 'not wonderful. I kind of went into automatic when it happened. I saw him, his head fell forward and I stumbled to the ground, but then I had somebody who potentially could have been alive, so I shouted to the gang downstairs. We started trying to do what we could, but it was hopeless. He had just . . .'

'I know,' said Clarissa. 'They made a good job of it. There wasn't anything you could do.'

'I just didn't see anyone either. I mean, I was driving about here the whole time and yet, I saw nobody there.'

'You blame yourself to a degree, don't you?'

'Well, yes. Maybe I should have seen someone other than the team. Maybe . . .'

'Don't,' said Clarissa. 'Whoever did this is cold. They're calculating and they clearly have something against Mr Epson. You did what you could. Sometimes it's not enough; sometimes there isn't anything to do. You need to go and talk to

41

somebody about it, though. I see this sort of thing a lot and I need to talk sometimes to a professional about it.'

The man nodded. 'I'll do that. I'm sorry to bother you, again.'

'Not at all,' said Clarissa. 'When you come with that attitude and a smile like that, you can talk to me any day.'

She watched the man give a nod and turn away. Clarissa wasn't getting any younger and the days of having someone around had long gone, but she wanted them back. She hungered for that companionship, somebody decent, someone just to be there, maybe. She turned back to her search advisor and smiled at her.

'Morrison is nice, isn't he? Better than that tosser of an airport manager.'

Clarissa went to speak, but there was a shout from across the airport fire ground. She could see someone in a blue overall pointing inside of the burnt-out vehicle. Clarissa strode over, her boots clipping across the asphalt, then she looked inside to see where the man was pointing. At the bottom of the car, she could see the metal, a little sliver barely visible.

'Shall I get it?' asked the man.

'No,' said Clarissa. 'No. Don't touch it.' Then she picked up her mobile phone, and dialled Jona Nakamura.

'Jona, love, we appear to have something out here. Looks like a knife inside one of the burnt-out cars at the fire ground. Looks pretty new and clean. Why don't you send one of your guys over, so we can tag and bag this properly? Also, get some photographs of where it is.'

After closing the call, she turned to the search advisor asking him to continue the search, but to cordon off that particular area while the forensic team gathered. As she finished speaking to him, Curtis James appeared beside her.

42

'What have you found? Is that what did it? Do you need a bag for that? Can we tell everybody that was the knife that did it?'

'Excuse me, you should get back in that car and get over to your office.'

The man stepped forward towards the burnt-out vehicle and then reached inside with his hand. Clarissa sprung forward, grabbed him by the shoulders, pulled him back, then took an arm and drove it up his back.

'That is enough,' she said. 'You go near that car again and I will do you for tampering with evidence. You need to leave here. You need to go back to your office or go home. Understand, you are a potential suspect.'

'Me? How can I be a suspect? I wasn't here. Why would I want this? You've closed the airport. I don't want my airport closed. My bosses are all over me, to get this place up and going again, making money. How can I be a suspect?'

'Because until we work out what's going on, just about everybody around here is a suspect on the airfield. I'm going to let your arm go.'

'Bloody hell, about time. That hurts.'

'If you don't go straight back to that car and to your office, I'll make sure it hurts. I'll also cuff you and I'll take you down to the station for obstructing a police investigation. When I'm done with you, Macleod will pay a visit, because compared to me, he's a Rottweiler.'

Clarissa was almost laughing inside, the Rottweiler Macleod, of course, he wasn't. She knew why she was on the team. She was the one who could go out and be a Rottweiler, but she also knew that Macleod could be more brutal in his own way. Whereas Clarissa might give the man the handcuffs treatment, lock him in a cell, Macleod would simply book him. Macleod would charge him almost dismissively. Clarissa let down the arm of Curtis James and he stood shaking it. Over Curtis's shoulder she could see Ian Morrison coming forward.

'Shall I take the airport manager back to his office?' he asked and Curtis shot him a glance that had daggers in it.

'That'd be most kind of you,' said Clarissa. 'If you could just come back after you escort Mr James into the car, there's something I'd like to ask you.'

Clarissa waited while Morrison took Curtis James back to the car, all the time receiving an earful from the airport manager about how he'd just been treated. When he returned, he smiled at Clarissa, almost laughing.

'Well, you've certainly made an impression on him. I don't think it's a good one from his point of view. But for the rest of the team that work here, it might be the best impression we've had in a long time.'

'I don't suffer fools, Mr Morrison, and frankly, that man's a fool.'

'Well, as he's out of earshot, I agree totally with you, but I'll never say it in front of him. I still have a job to keep. You wanted something from me?'

'Not from you, just a recommendation. Where's good to eat?'

'Go down to Tobermory; there's a number of nice restaurants down the front.' Ian passed a few details.

'I guess you'll be off home tonight, little wife to keep you well fed. You'll have somebody to talk to then about what happened?'

Ian gave a half grin and cocked his head towards Clarissa. 'Not very subtle,' he said. 'It's just me at home. Used to be my daughter as well, but she finally got herself married and was off.'

'Well,' said Clarissa, 'and obviously, I'm giving you this from a purely professional point of view, if you're struggling with what happened and you need someone to talk to, here's my card.'

'Shouldn't you really not be talking to me too much until you're sure I'm not one of the guilty party?'

'Well, you can't be,' said Clarissa. 'You were out here, so you certainly didn't kill him and I am still being professional. I mean what I say, if you need someone to talk to, I'm here, you can talk to me. Anything beyond that, will have to wait until after the case.'

Ian Morrison took the card, looked at the number and then gave Clarissa a smile. 'You're pretty forward,' he said.

'Well, we're at that stage in life where you don't want to hang around too long, do you? Besides, if this is solved in two or three days, I'm right out of here back to Inverness.'

'And what? Never to be seen again?' asked Ian.

'Well, that's why I'm seeing if there is anything to come back for. If you need to chat, I'm here. Now if you'll excuse me,' said Clarissa, 'I see the forensic wagon arriving at the fire ground. Do me a favour; keep that man away from me.'

Ian Morrison laughed, 'I'll do my best, but in fairness, I don't think he'll want to tackle you again.'

Chapter 6

Macleod was almost on tiptoes as he stood outside the forensic van awaiting Jona Nakamura, Inverness station's main forensic officer. Part of him saw a quick solution. Would there be fingerprints on the knife? Maybe some DNA, something that would tag the killer, so they could arrest and all go home.

For all that solving crimes was his life, Macleod was becoming less and less keen to be away from his beloved Jane back in Inverness, and though she never complained when he did have to go on his travels, he knew she was missing him too. The question of retirement was always looming with him. *When should you give up? Should it be when the next person was ready to take over?* A highly unselfish attitude, except that it was kind of selfish to himself not thinking about Jane.

How could you judge when someone was ready to take over? Was he ready when he became a DI, in the many years, pounding the streets in Glasgow, had seen other detective inspectors in front of him, learned from them, as Hope had from him. And yet something within him said she wasn't ready. Maybe it was just a fear or maybe it was because he wanted her to be too like him. That was unfair, he realised that, but it still brought him

46

around to that question of retirement.

Ross had once asked him what he would do when he retired; surely this was his life. Macleod had thought, *If my life consists of finding out who killed people, it's a pretty grim one. The need to exist based upon other people's need to kill.* No, he was more than that and with Jane, he felt comfortable in their life. They liked to tour, they liked to go and see places of interest, go for walks, have a decent lunch together. There was plenty he could occupy himself with, most of it, far less dark than what his days normally were taken up with.

The trouble was that when the question came up, he was never sure. Jane said to him, 'When are we ever sure of anything? When are we ever one hundred percent?' He hadn't been sure when he first got together with Jane. He hadn't been sure about Hope when she was first assigned with him; in fact, in some ways, he'd rejected her. Ross, with his sexuality, was far different to Macleod's, and had also been a sticking point initially. Macleod had adapted, and he wouldn't trade Ross away for the world. That was the problem—you were never sure. The question with retirement was, if you made a mistake, could you pop back a year or two later?

The rear door of the forensic wagon opened, and Jona Nakamura stepped down, holding a knife within a plastic bag.

'One of these days, you're going to bring me a weapon and on it is going to actually be a signature from the killer saying, "This is me. I did it."'

Macleod's heart sank. 'You're telling me you didn't get anything from it, aren't you?'

'Weapon's been cleaned, inspector but I can tell you some things. This is the knife that was used to cut the throat. It matches exactly. It's a very sharp blade, so to my mind, they didn't have to have that much strength to be able to whip it across the neck. By the looks of it, there wasn't that much of a struggle from Mr Epson. A reasonable hand on the shoulder, holding him firm while they quickly cut his throat. I do reckon that they held him in position. The downside of that was, they were probably wearing gloves because I can't get any fingerprints. They may have covered up their hair because I can't find any on Mr Epson. There are plenty around the floor, but then again, people work in there. It would not be unusual to find the DNA of anyone who'd been working there over the last six months, especially when they're in and out on a fairly consistent basis.'

'So now we've found the "where" of the murder weapon; it's over a short distance away from the tower. Basically, all you can tell me is, "Yes, that's the murder weapon."'

'Well, not just that, Inspector. You see, it was cleaned. The cleaning fluid that was used on it came from the tower, in the cleaner's cupboard.'

'I take it you've been in there then?'

'Well, I have. I can only find the cleaner's DNA. Whoever did it were fairly clean. Either that, or they may have stepped right into the corridor to clean it, and then put the cleaning equipment back into the cupboard, with gloves on, doing it quickly. They didn't leave any trace if that's what they did do.'

'You're not filling me with a lot of optimism, Jona,' said Macleod. 'As much as this is a nice island, I was kind of hoping to get back for the weekend.'

'Jane got tickets for something?'

'No. In fact, we weren't doing anything particular.'

'Well, then, that's good,' said Jona. 'Shows that you don't need to be entertained; you're enough for each other. Kind of sweet, really.'

'Stop it,' said Macleod, 'and I'll thank you for not mentioning that to anyone else, especially as you haven't brought me the killer.'

'We'll continue, but we're just about done. I'm not sure where else to look at. I'm happy to stay for a while, but if nothing else turns up, there doesn't seem to be a point in the forensic team being here. They can always come back.'

'Give it a day or so,' said Macleod. 'Anyway, maybe Ross will have better luck. Our killer must have gone over to the fire ground, and I would suspect they'd do it pretty quickly. He's working the CCTV, so I think the least we should get, is a height or possibly the sex of the killer. Be able to trace who's coming in and out as well.'

'You know what I like about you,' said Jona, 'it's that endless optimism.'

'I think you mistake optimism for a desire to go home.'

'Yes,' said Jona, 'I think I do.'

Macleod thanked the forensic officer, then turned and walked over to the airport terminal where every security officer he passed simply nodded at him. The word had clearly got out not to annoy Macleod. Inside, he gave a wry smile. One thing he was aware of was his team around him were fiercely loyal to him and protective. Clarissa Urquhart, while she would tease him, was the first one to stand in line to stop anyone getting near him. Hope would follow suit.

Ross had located himself in the security office, where he was able to see where the cameras scanned from the airport building. He'd been rerunning the records, checking to make sure who had gone in and out of the building on the day and around the time of the murder. As Macleod walked into the room, Ross kept his eyes low, giving a gentle, 'Sir.'

'That's not good news, is it?' said Macleod.

'No, sir. It's not. You'd better take a seat so I can explain.'

Macleod pulled up a chair, and sat down with his hands in his pockets.

'I don't think we're going to solve this one quickly. You see, we've got CCTV at the tower. We've got it also operating from the apron from the airport building and around various areas and the fence. We know that our killer dispatched Mr Epson and then got over at some point to the fire ground where they dropped the knife. They also went via the cleaning cupboard.'

'And you're going to tell me that there's no cameras for those routes?'

'No, sir. There are cameras for those routes and up until lunchtime of that day, they would have caught our killer marching across, but someone came in and moved them. I spoke to the security people here, and to be honest, they're not that bothered about the airfield. You've got air traffic and they're watching for what's going on. Security are more concerned with the terminal building and people on the apron getting into the aircraft. That's very much where they see the danger area as being; air traffic are the ones watching beyond. Yet at night, it's so dark that you're not going to see much from that tower.'

'Especially not if you're dead,' said Macleod.

'Well, that too. The fire ground has lights, but they weren't on because they only use them if they're out there at night training.'

'So, what did happen?'

'Someone came in here at about lunchtime on the day of the murder and turned every camera away. They were still focusing on areas of the airfield, but the direct line from the tower to the fire ground was not covered. To be honest, the security people probably wouldn't have noticed because they don't look at those. When I came in originally, and I was being shown through it by the security staff, the first thing they said to me was, 'Here's the apron camera. Here's this camera showing a plane. Here's this camera at the gate,' and to be honest, I had to actually point out where the airfield ones were to them. All they said to me was, 'Well, we don't really look at those because it's not what we cover.''

'How well known is that?' said Macleod.

'I did ask, and they said very well known. The system in here, it doesn't have a lockout, as long as you can get into this room, you're fine.'

'So, who came into this room at that time?'

'Unknown,' said Ross, 'the problem we've got is that the interior camera recording sweeps across, it spends two minutes going out to the left and then it sweeps back and does another two minutes on the right and then sweeps back again. If you were in here for any length of time, or out there in the departure area, you'd see that, you'd know that's what the camera was doing, so it would be very easy to time and come in through the front door, make sure the camera was on the left-hand side and then make your way to that security office, pop in, change it. Wait another couple of minutes, come back out when the camera is away and disappear. The other problem is, of course, that they could have been in the terminal already. In fact, if you're good, you could actually have got up off your seat, gone and done it and got back before the camera would pick up that you'd moved.'

'Any idea why they would choose lunchtime?' asked

Macleod.

'Three flights in, the busiest time of the day,' said Ross. 'These people know what they're about; whoever did it knows how the place works.'

'Do you think we're looking at someone on the airfield then? Control staff, maybe someone from the terminal building?'

'I think it's the controllers and the staff from the tower.'

'Why do you think that?' asked Macleod.

'It's the setup. I've said you could walk through here. You could time it. You could use your two minutes, but people would still see you here. What I've found out is that the feed for the cameras that are over on the airfield and based around the airfield run through the telecommunications room at the bottom of the tower. If you go in there, you are able to actually change them from there.'

'Do we know that's where they were changed from?'

'No, sir. Because whichever end you change it from, it doesn't record it. They're just two units sending in the same signals, and it doesn't record which unit is used.'

'What you're saying,' said Macleod, 'is that you've got one system doing all the recording, but you can actually change the camera inputs from two different control stations, neither of which are identified specifically?'

'That's correct,' said Ross. 'Like I say, I think our best bet is to focus on the tower, because if you were in and out of here in the security room, people would see. I've asked about and we can't find anyone untoward going in, so unless the security crew have changed it . . .'

'The killing is at the tower so best we start there,' said Macleod.

'My thoughts exactly,' said Ross.

'So, I'm going to need to work out who was in the tower that day.'

'Already done for you, sir. Four people were in that tower that day, as well as John Epson. Firstly, there's two controllers, Zoe Jillings and Harold Lyme, they're the morning and the day shift. John Epson's the night shift. Both of them would be away between three o'clock and six o'clock that night. That means that any of them could have gone down and changed the controls at lunchtime.

'There was also the assistant that was in, Kylie Youngs. Kylie came in at an unusual time, in that she didn't start off the day because they had a sick assistant, so Kylie stretched her shift and covered across a longer pattern than she was used to, but she was out of there by six o'clock that night. However, she was also in during lunchtime, so Kylie had the ability to do that.'

'Anyone else? You said four.'

'Sarah Pullet, she's the cleaner. She normally comes in just after eleven, works through over lunch and then away again. Oh, and the other person that was in was the airport manager.'

'Curtis James? He's not been endearing himself to me.'

Macleod saw Ross smirk. 'Clarissa had said the same; I think she might go for him before we are done as well. One of the things about him is he doesn't look a shape to be able to commit the killing, get down the stairs, and go across the airfield. Not the most dynamic of men.'

'No, but when needs must, Ross, I've seen people less fit than him commit murder.'

'I wasn't suggesting we rule him out, sir. I was just saying that he's not exactly the fittest. I'm struggling to see him as the murderer.'

53

'Do we know when they all left?'

'Yes,' said Ross, 'the car park CCTV was still on the car park. Now the controllers have to go and park up, then enter airside and walk across to the tower; it's just inside. You have an issue that they're always seen arriving, and they're always seen departing. One of the security actually said that Curtis wanted it that way.'

'Recently?'

'No, he said about six months ago. I think he was doing a time check on them.'

'He sounds the type,' said Macleod, 'he really does. Hope's going to be back soon, so we'll start setting up some interviews. It will be tomorrow at best. Jona has confirmed the knife is what killed John Epson, but she's found no DNA, hair, or anything else on it. She's struggling to come up with anyone. It looks like we're going to have to get into the minutia of how this place worked. Who had cause? Who had motive? Who didn't like who?'

'Very good, sir,' said Ross. 'No quick return then.'

'I'm afraid not, Ross. Anyway, good work. Keep at it and see what else you can bring me. If you can, find out all you can about Curtis James. The man interests me. He may not be the murderer but he sure as heck could be a catalyst.

Chapter 7

At the hotel that evening, Macleod had reviewed the interviews for the next morning, keen to get those who had been in the tower that day spoken to and assessed. He decided that Hope would visit Zoe Jillings while he would take Howard Lyme and Kylie Youngs, leaving Clarissa Urquhart to talk to Sarah Pullet, the cleaner, before they would move on to the rest.

Hope was up and out of the hotel by eight o'clock in the morning, making her way around to Kelliemor where she found Zoe's house beside the sea. It was picturesque, the rocks splashed upon by the approaching tide, and although the air was cold, the sun had come out. Even though it was low in the sky, Hope could feel the warmth from it, and watched the house as it was bathed in nature's splendour.

As Hope walked up the driveway, stones crunching underneath her feet, she noticed several potted plants here and there; then she saw some fairy houses, cute creations. She thought she saw dreamcatchers, dangling chimes that were still due to the lack of wind. As she approached the front door, there were drapes beside a glass panel, multiple colours.

Hope rapped on the door, wondering just who Zoe Jillings

was. The front door opened to a woman that stood about half a foot smaller than Hope but who was eminently more colourful. Her long black hair had clearly not been brushed this morning, but it surrounded a chubby if cheerful face. Hope noted the number of piercings through the ears and nose and even down to the lip.

'I'm Detective Sergeant Hope McGrath here to interview you. I take it you got the message from DC Ross.'

'Yes, it's quite early though, isn't it? I'm afraid I only got up twenty minutes ago because I knew you were coming. If you hadn't have warned me, I wouldn't have been up at all, but come on, in you come.'

Hope stepped forward onto an orange carpet and almost felt a sense of nausea from the colour. A small dog yapped at her feet chasing around at her ankles, making Hope want to just kick him. Maybe it was the hour of the day that shortened her patience with the animal. Zoe Jillings led the way through to her kitchen where Hope saw joss sticks burning. For a woman that had only been up twenty minutes, there seemed to be a number of candles and other meditation items working overtime.

'Do you want tea? I'm afraid it's not going to be any of the normal stuff. I've got different infusions and that.'

'You don't have any coffee, do you?' asked Hope.

'Don't touch that stuff, don't like it going into me. Then you get the other ones, the decaf. They use chemicals in some of them. I don't like chemicals in my body.'

Hope noted the cigarette papers at the side for rolling but couldn't see any tobacco. The overall impression was that the woman would probably roll up a joint, but she'd probably have the wisdom not to do it while Hope was there. Zoe was wearing a long skirt, multicoloured, and a top that looked like she'd slept in it, which was probably correct.

'Two days ago, you were at work. Correct?' asked Hope.

'Yes. I was the morning shift, so I was quite tired, but yes, I was in.'

'Did you see John Epson that day?'

'Briefly. He came in for the afternoon hours, and I disappeared about half an hour later.'

'You said hello?'

'I always said hello to John. You couldn't help but like John.'

'When you said you liked John, did you spend much time with him?'

'Well, no, if I'm honest,' said Zoe as she reached over and pressed a button on her kettle. 'You see the thing about John is, he's one of those people that's harmless. I liked him in the sense that he could give a bit of stick to the management and that, but he was very moralistic. He wouldn't have appreciated any of this stuff. Not that he ever said anything. We were just two people that didn't hit it off. We worked fine together as colleagues, we could discuss what was going on at the airfield if needed, but frankly, he was quite boring. Do you understand what I mean?'

'Maybe,' said Hope. 'He was quite a bit older than you, wasn't he?'

'Hell, yes. Much older than me. I think that was part of the problem. He didn't get most of the way people see things now. He may have been brought up in the more traditional-type churches rather than a living-your-life-now mentality. You just do what you want. Do it your way. I don't think he liked that, but he was decent enough. He never complained at me.'

'I take it you were shocked when you found out he'd been

57

killed.'

'Well, it still is a shock. It's a bit of a brutal way to go, isn't it? Why kill somebody? Over what?'

'Did you know anything about his outside life? Outside of work?'

'No. He never talked much about it either. We didn't really talk. We talked if we had to. For instance, there was a debate about one of the taxiways and how they were creating it and what height the signs needed to be. We got involved, the two of us. We worked quite happily together on that, but as soon as work talk was done, that was it. We didn't even discuss what we were having for our lunch together, never mind what he did with his life.'

'Okay,' said Hope. 'On the day that you were there, did you at any point visit the telecommunications room downstairs?'

'I don't believe so. We don't tend to go in there unless you need to make a recording.'

'A recording?' asked Hope. 'What do you mean?'

'All the radiotelephony, the RT, from the tower is recorded. Sometimes, if there's been an incident or a minor occurrence, you might have to go in. If you're training someone, you might have to pop down and listen to the RT. If you're the local assessor, you might go down there to listen, check up on the standard of RT that's being used. Other than that, we don't tend to go in. The telecommunications engineers when they come, which is not that often, that's their domain and they don't like people having been in.'

'You're telling me,' said Hope, 'you weren't in on that day.'

'No.'

'Okay,' said Hope, and watched as the woman poured herself a cup of water and dropped some type of herb into it. 'So, you're not aware if John Epson had any enemies?'

'Well, I'm not aware of anyone who wanted to kill him,' said Zoe, 'but I can tell you this, him and old Curtis, they never saw eye-to-eye.'

'You mean, Curtis James, the airport manager?'

'Yes, Curtis James. The thing was that Eppy and Curtis never saw eye-to-eye because frankly, Curtis is incompetent—Eppy wasn't. Eppy was a good controller. He could do his job well and could pick out issues coming up. The trouble was that Curtis didn't like issues coming up for two reasons. One, he'd have to do something about them. Two, he genuinely didn't understand what the problem was.'

'Were they too technical, more kind of air traffic-type things?' asked Hope.

'No, he's just thick.'

'That's quite a statement,' said Hope. 'You're able to back that up.'

'With numerous examples. Time and again Curtis and Eppy were at loggerheads. You see, the rest of us, we would turn around, we'd say to Curtis, 'Look, that's wrong,' and he would go away, but Eppy would go off the handle at him. Eppy would hunt him down, and on some things that weren't really that important. Yes, technically it was wrong, but it worked, it was safe enough, but those Eppy would go after. Now, if something was point blank unsafe, well, I wouldn't do it, and the other controllers wouldn't do it. We'd get together and we'd win our case over him, but Eppy went after him on everything, and hence, Curtis did not like him.'

'When you say not like him,' asked Hope, 'how badly?'

'I'm not saying he would kill him for it. I mean, Curtis is the boss as he likes to call himself. Technically his word goes unless you refer it to the CAA, the Civil Aviation Authority, and they slap his wrist for it. Is there anything you need?' asked Zoe. 'It's just that I could really do with a shower to wake up a bit. I mean you're welcome to come up and chat to me while I'm in the shower.'

'Probably not the best,' said Hope. 'Why don't you go up and have your shower and I'll wait, see if I've got any more questions? You're not going to be long, are you?'

'Ten to fifteen minutes at the most. Sorry, I just feel I could do with a clean. I'm not good at this time of the morning, I really am not.'

'It's okay,' said Hope, 'I understand.'

Zoe Jillings whirled away out of the kitchen, and Hope could hear her going up the stairs. Hope strode round into the living room of the house, and started looking around at the items that were there. There were trinkets, little bits and pieces from the Far East. She also saw several photographs of often reasonably large gatherings, somewhat hedonistic in nature. Not that they shocked Hope because she was quite open about people and their lifestyles, but she was rather more interested in just who Zoe was.

On several occasions, she saw a group of women together, usually on a beach somewhere out in the wild. Hope was able to pick up that Zoe had her arm around this woman or that, and she rarely saw any photographs of men in the house. There were occasional ones, one or two with her arm draped around them, but it did look more like pals than anything else.

A couple of the photographs with the women made Hope think that possibly Zoe had a greater affinity for women than men. It was as she was looking at one of the photographs that Zoe walked into the room behind her. Hope turned and nearly stopped in her tracks because Zoe was standing there, her black hair now wet and hanging down her back. But what really took Hope by surprise was the simple towel wrapped around the woman. It certainly wasn't a bath towel.

'Sorry,' said Zoe. 'I thought I should come down as quick as I could so you could get away.'

'There's really no rush,' said Hope. 'You can go and dress. Please, go and put something on.' The woman ignored Hope and walked over to some of the photographs, picking up one in particular which saw Zoe on a beach with a number of other women.

'That's my kind of lifestyle,' said Zoe. 'You look like somebody who would enjoy that too.'

'I'm afraid I don't really get out to do that sort of thing anymore, duty calls too often,' said Hope. 'Tell me, did you notice anything unusual about anyone else who was in that day? Harold or Kylie Youngs? Even Sarah Pullet? I figure Curtis was over as well.'

'Harold was Harold as usual; we get on fine. Kylie is a bit dim, but she's okay as an assistant. To be honest, I don't really know Sarah that well, but you said Curtis was over. You're right with that. That was the problem with him. It's what really annoyed Eppy.'

'How do you mean?'

'Eppy always saw the control tower as ours; this is the side we work. Curtis doesn't. Curtis thinks he owns everything, which I guess technically he does, but he doesn't understand what we do. He kept coming over. He would come up to the tower, you'd be sitting there, and all of a sudden, you hear the thump, thump, thump coming up the metal stairs. I'd turn around to say hello to him if the traffic wasn't busy. You know what he did? He would stand and he'd just pull his trousers up. All the time, hands down inside, pulling a shirt down and then trousers up. I mean who does that, especially in front of a woman? There's a name for men like that.'

'Did he ever try anything on with you?

'Oh, yes. Well, I say yes but it's nothing so explicit. He's too scared for that; someone might have a go back at him. Instead, what Curtis does is he tries to get close to you, tries to make the little puns and jabs and see if you're interested. Well, I mean come on, I'm not that desperate.'

Hope laughed. 'I think he's been causing havoc with our staff as well,' said Hope. 'I know he isn't endearing himself either. How badly do you think he wants his own way though?' Hope asked, becoming rather serious. She noticed that Zoe was drifting towards her more.

'I think he's quite keen; he doesn't take rejection well. Then again, I think he caught on after a while with me.'

'In what way do you mean?' asked Hope.

'Well, men aren't really my thing. Are they?'

'I didn't get that feeling,' said Hope. 'Did he have a problem with that?'

'I'm thinking more of a problem with being rejected than actually with what sort of sexuality I have. To be honest, I think his mind would probably enjoy the idea of me and another woman.'

Hope stepped back, turned around and looked out the window of the house as much to put some space between herself and Zoe because suddenly she seemed to be drifting towards her. 'I'm not sure how much else I've got to ask you,' said Hope. 'Have you ever used the CCTV systems on the airfield?'

'Don't touch them. Wouldn't go near; that's Tels' stuff. Like I say, you don't go near it; they get quite irate with you.'

'I don't know when your airport is going to open again,' said Hope, 'but we'll be in touch. I might need to talk to you further, make some proper statements down at the station.'

'Well, I'm here,' she said. 'If you want to stay for a half hour or so, not tell your boss, you can join me in a little spliff if you want.'

'Do you smoke those when you're working?' asked Hope.

'Of course not. They don't know I do any of this sort of stuff at the airfield, and I don't do it on the days I'm working. You have to be clear of mind. If you got caught having alcohol in your system or any of this stuff on the day you actually work, you'd lose your licence. It's not the greatest job, but you know what? It pays well and it's given me this house and has given me a lifestyle I can afford, so I don't chuck it away. It's all for recreational use the stuff I'm going to smoke; there's nothing that you need to worry about.'

'I'm sure there isn't,' said Hope. 'Just be available if we need you.'

Hope walked towards the door and found Zoe Jillings following close behind. Her hand was holding on to the towel now, as Hope reckoned the size of it, it couldn't have been that easy a fit. As she exited and began to make her way down the path towards the car, Zoe stepped out of the front door and shouted after her.

'If someone needs to talk to me again, will it be you?'

'Can't say,' said Hope. 'Really can't say, depends what we need to talk to you about, but don't worry, we'll let you know.'

Hope walked down to the car. When she got inside, she looked back up to the house and saw Zoe Jillings still standing there at the front door. She felt a little off. The woman was very overt in some ways, but Hope also felt the falseness from it. There was one thing to be overt, but actually, most people, if they really liked you, could be quite cagey, not wanting to blow the moment. She felt as if Zoey was putting on a front, trying to make out that she had an interest in Hope. As she started the engine and spun the car around, Hope really had no idea of just how the woman stood in terms of the whole investigation.

Chapter 8

Macleod pulled into an estate on the west side of Tobermory, up from the sea and one that looked reasonably modern. The house he parked up in front of was large and he could see an extension at the rear. Howard Lyme clearly had money, but then again, he was an air traffic controller, and they were paid well so maybe it wasn't that surprising.

After parking on the street, Macleod walked up the stone slates in the driveway, staying off the stones either side of him, and approached the front door before ringing the bell. It played a Christmas tune, which Macleod thought was a little out of season, but nonetheless, he stepped back and glanced around the door seeing some dishevelled curtains behind it.

The curtains were thrown back, the door opened, and a woman in a bright yellow t-shirt stood looking at him.

'Not today, love. You'll not get much luck with door-to-door around here.'

Macleod gave a quick glance down at his black tie and jacket and wondered just how many door-to-door salesmen were left.

'I'm afraid I'm not selling. I'm here on a rather more serious matter. I'm Detective Inspector Seoras Macleod, and I need to speak to Harold Lyme. Have I got the correct house?'

'Yes. Harold's here. Just a moment.' The woman turned and shouted up the stairs behind her. 'Harold, it's the police. Probably be about Eppy.'

A rather tall man came down the stairs. In his arms was a baby, while around his neck was another small child. He seemed to be laughing as he came down and the boy attached to him was making a good impression of strangling him.

'I'm Detective Inspector Macleod, Mr Lyme. I'm sorry to bother you at home, but I do need to speak to you.'

'Of course, you do, Inspector. Just a moment. I'll get these monkeys off me.'

Macleod stepped back from the door, but the woman ushered him in. 'No, no, no, no. Through to the back. There's a little sunroom out there. Be ideal for you. I'm Jenny Lyme, by the way.'

The woman extended her hand, which Macleod shook, and he thanked her before she led him through the house. Everywhere he looked, there were toys or drawings on the wall done by their kids. It looked like a crazily busy family home, something Macleod didn't have a lot of experience of, and when he reached the sunroom, which was noticeably tidier, he was somewhat relieved.

'Now you sit down there, Inspector, and I'll fix you a cup of tea, or is it something else?'

'If you've got a coffee, that would be great,' said Macleod, 'but only if it's no trouble.'

'It's no trouble at all, Inspector. It's not often we see your sort over here. Terrible thing with Eppy. Nice man. Just terrible. Anyway, I'll leave you to discuss that with Harold. I'll just go get this kettle on. Do you want the good stuff?' The woman gave a Macleod a wink. 'I mean coffee. You look like a man who likes the good stuff when it comes to coffee.'

Harold entered in through the door. 'Jenny, don't be ridiculous. Just give the man the good stuff. He's our guest. A bit of that cake you made as well.'

Harold Lyme sat down on a large wicker chair and stared across at Macleod. 'Now she's left, it's a terrible business. I only told her that Eppy had died. I didn't say how.'

'Well, we didn't officially release it either,' said Macleod. 'Not yet. It'll come out though. Was she close to him at all?'

'No, she'd only met him once or twice on a work's do. Jenny's just quite fond of everyone. One of those people in life who's just bubbly, keen to help everyone. That's why I like her so much. She's a great wife. No airs or graces, no frills about her. Jenny just gets done what needs done and we take care of each other. That's the important thing, Inspector, isn't it?'

Macleod gave a nod. 'If only everyone was like that,' he said, 'but I need to talk to you about Mr Epson. How long had you known John?'

'Well, he's been in that airport ever since I knew. I've been there now, oh, ten years. Used to work down the area centres but moved up for a bit of a quieter life and now have a family. Met Jenny down in London, but we came up here and now we've got seven kids. The job up here is a little bit less taxing than it is down there. Not as well paid, but that's not the important side of things, is it?'

'Indeed not,' said Macleod, 'but I was asking about Mr Epson. You said you'd known him ten years. What sort of man was he?'

'Well,' said Harold, as his wife entered through the door, 'the thing about John was, he was quite principled, a very upright man. A decent fella, but very much on his high horse when it came to things being done right. He could go for the jugular. A good thing in an air traffic controller though.'

Jenny placed some cake down in front of Macleod before taking some coffee off a tray, pouring it for him, and handing it to him. 'Do you remember the to-do?' she said, 'about the knife and forks?'

'Oh, yes,' said Harold, 'Christmas party. Wait till you hear this. So, we're all sat down and the place we'd gone to obviously was making an effort this Christmas, but the soup spoons, the knives, and the forks, they just were not to John's liking. Apparently, they were laid out in the wrong order.'

'How big a meal was it?' asked Macleod.

'This is the thing. It's a Christmas do, you know? We don't care. We're just there for the grub and a bit of fun but John takes a look at it, and he says something to the manager. Now, if the manager had the good sense, he'd have just gone, 'Ah, yeah, lovely,' walked away and that would've been that, but no, he tries to tell John he's wrong. So, John gets up on his high horse. It never comes to anything much, but John's there for half an hour with this guy. Meanwhile, dinner's not getting served, but that was the thing about John. He didn't care.'

There was a scream from upstairs followed by a large thud.

'Oh, heck,' said Jenny, 'I'll go and see to that, not to disturb you. Here, I'll close the door after me. Very nice to meet you, Inspector.'

'Well, thank you for the coffee and the cake looks great, much appreciated.' Macleod watched the woman leave the room before turning back to Harold. 'What happened on the day in question?' asked Macleod.

'Well, that was the thing. I handed over to Eppy. I was day shift; Zoe was morning shift. I don't know if you've met her, very different from John. Very New Age-y, a good worker though. We get on fine, can do her job, but yeah, different. Anyway, I came in for the day shift, so I'd have been in around eight-thirty, Zoe's in for six-thirty, John comes in around about half-one, two-ish. Zoe would have seen him for about an hour. They come in and have a natter. It depends how quiet it is. When we're not busy upstairs we just sit and chat. Of course, that was the day we had the assistant off. We also had Kylie in and she's something else, a little bit on the excitable side. Only nineteen, but don't get me wrong, I'm as much of a man as anyone else. Lovely looking girl but very forward and for a married man, one to keep at a distance.

'Did John keep her at a distance?'

'John wouldn't have been for that type of woman; as I said, he was very proper. So, anyway, he came in and he was taking over. I had done my second stint of the day, John comes in, does the first bit of the afternoon, I then take over for a couple of hours in the evening, and then John is doing the last bit. Now I'd have left about six-ish, Kylie is probably away not long after me, and John was left on his own because we're short.

'There's not that many flights at the end of the day, so John can handle it without my assistant. He also knows how to do all the weather, as we all do. That was the best result, to bring Kylie in to cover the middle of the day when we're busier. We opened without her; John closed without her too.'

'So, you said you went home at six? You didn't return, did you?'

'No. I was back here.'

69

'Can your wife vouch for you being here that evening?'

'She can vouch for me coming back and getting my dinner; after that, I went out for a walk. It's my custom at that sort of time. You see I'm there for about ten hours so when I come back, I want to chill out or take a walk, and this place is not always the quietest in the evening. Jenny is good in that way, she took care of the kids, I went off for a walk, I was back here around about, oh, ten . . . no, nine. Nine would be right.'

'When did you go out for the walk?' asked Macleod.

'Seven-ish.'

'That's unfortunate. It doesn't give you an alibi then for when John was killed.'

'You don't seriously think I had something to do with it? I got on fine with John.'

'I'm not saying anything,' said Macleod. 'I have to try and rule people out though.' We don't just look at people and think, ''Yes, they're a decent person; they'll never do it.' A little bit of evidence saying that you were unable to have been in that tower at that time of night would be good. However, do you know if John had any issues with anybody else at work?'

'Well, Julia Fluke. She's one of the controllers that wasn't on that day. She and John didn't see eye to eye. I know previously, when I'd been in a couple of days before, they'd been having quite heated discussions down below. I was up on the desk, and I think Julia was the morning controller—John was the evening. This was around the middle of the day; they were downstairs and I heard heated words but I don't know what it was about. It could be about a controlling issue. Julia is probably a little more relaxed than John would be. She would say free-wheeling.'

'And John didn't like that? Did you ever hear him accuse her of anything or make any comment like that?'

'No. Like I said, it was all quite heated, but I was upstairs. I remember I turned to Kylie and sort of raised my eyebrows at the time.'

'Okay,' said Macleod. 'Anybody else have any issues with John?'

'Well, if I'm honest, I have to say that Curtis did. Do you know Curtis James, our airport manager?'

Macleod nodded and tried not to screw up his face and so influence his witness.

'Well, Curtis is a bit of an arse, to be honest. He comes over all the time marching into us to do this, to do that. You look at the stuff and you think, 'Actually, do you know what? That's wrong. He can't do this, that's illegal, this is not right, that would end up with an aircraft possibly crashing or coming very close to it. I mean, quite honestly, he's treated with a lot of contempt by most of the controllers. The thing is that Eppy was the more vocal amongst us, whereas the rest of us would just write on a piece of paper, 'This is wrong,' da da da da, throw it back at him. Eppy would go and see him, and Eppy wouldn't be behind the door in telling him he was an idiot.'

'How did Curtis react to that?'

'How does Curtis react to anything? Off in a huff. The other problem was, you see, that Curtis used to come over and Eppy wouldn't like it, because Curtis'd come and try and talk to Kylie while the work was going on, upstairs in the tower. He'd stand there and oh, you could see his tongue hanging out. Like I said to you, Kylie, a lovely looking girl, but you don't go near someone like that as a married man. Curtis is old enough to be her grandad.'

'Was there anything going on between them?'

'I have no idea, Inspector; this is my life outside of work. I don't go out and see what anybody else is doing.'

'Were there any rumours?'

'There's always rumours. Rumours about a lot of things. There were once rumours about me and Sarah Pullet, the cleaner, all complete rubbish. Fortunately, Jenny knows that but people make rumours out of nothing. The rumour with Sarah came about because her grandmother had died and I was the first one she'd met in work. She ended up crying on my shoulder, but people make things out of that, don't they? Now, Curtis and Eppy, most of the things they argued on were about work and it was par for the course. If I'm honest, I don't see Curtis getting that annoyed because frankly, if that was what was driving him to have a go at Eppy in that way, we'd all be at risk.'

'It's just something I need to be aware of,' said Macleod. 'These things sometimes happen for the smallest of reasons, people's minds snap. They just feel humiliated.'

'Well, Curtis will never feel humiliated; his ego is to too big for that. Now get that cake down you,' said the man, almost getting into a bit of a flurry. 'If we don't, she'll wonder what's wrong with it. Oh, she's great, but sometimes she delves too deep about things. Keen on her baking, likes everybody to enjoy it.'

Macleod picked up the small fork, and cut into his cake, taking a mouthful. He'd seen the icing on top with the lime around it, and when he put it into his mouth, he knew it was carrot cake. He was going to put it back down having had a small bite and continue his questioning but it was good. He put half of it in his mouth, chewed and had a drink of coffee before asking another question.

'If you're alone at night up in that tower,' said Macleod, 'how easy is it to know when somebody is coming up?'

'We've got the metal stairs there, and a clank, clank, clank, clank, we usually hear it. It's awkward though. I mean, there are noises you hear if it's very still; we hear noises all the time. I quite like to have the TV or something on if I'm on my own for a bit of company. Your mind wanders, doesn't it, Inspector? Then you start hearing noises? That day was quite windy as there was quite a weather front coming through. If I remember correctly, it was quite hard to hear when it's like that. Quite a noise from outside. It also depends if you've got the phones on.'

'You mean the headset?' asked Macleod.

'Yes, we've got the big, old ones, not the new modern ones, quite small around the ears, but these ones we've got, clamp around the ears. There's a cutting in it because you're meant be able to hear everybody in the room as well but a lot of us wear them with one ear off, which makes it quite interesting because, you see, sometimes you're talking on the phone and on the radiotelephony as well. And that means that one comes through one ear, and one comes through the other if they're both on. You have to remember to put it back on.'

'So, in short, with Eppy, he'd have heard someone coming up the stairs.'

'I'd have thought so, but I could understand if he didn't,' said Harold. Macleod reached over for his cake, polishing it off before having another drink of the coffee which he realised, wasn't bad either.

'Thank you for your time,' said Macleod. 'I may have more to ask, but please don't go anywhere over the next few days.'

'I have seven kids to be here and look after. I'm not going

anywhere,' said Harold. 'I guess Curtis's pushing you to get the airfield open again.'

'What makes you say that?'

'Curtis rang me, actually asked if you were allowed to do that.'

'What did you tell him?' asked Macleod.

'I told him to go get a lawyer. I don't know. You're the police. I assume you can come in and close anywhere down, especially if you've got forensic people on the case. Besides that, I told him you're investigating a murder. You're not going to care about the next flight in.'

'I have a feeling that your Mr James would not be so wise about our procedures,' said Macleod.

'Oh, you better believe it.'

Chapter 9

Clarissa Urquhart walked along the busy street until she saw the flat above the shop. The wooden door had the correct number on it for the flat but it seemed to be half off of its hinges. Clarissa was wondering how it locked at all. There was a little plastic buzzer by the left-hand side and Clarissa pressed it, waiting for an answer. When none came, she rapped the door with her hand, gradually getting louder, waiting for someone to answer it.

'I'm coming, just hold on.'

Clarissa heard the click of the lock, and the door was half dragged backwards, as it scraped along the floor. Clearly, one hinge was missing. In front of her stood a girl of roughly equal height, but with short blonde hair. In some ways Clarissa thought she was quite shy, almost retreating, but from her eyes, there was a piercing stare.

'Who are you?'

'I'm Detective Sergeant Clarissa Urquhart. I'm looking for Sarah Pullet.'

'Well, that's me. I'm a bit busy now.'

'And I'm very busy,' said Clarissa, 'with the dead body we found at the airport. I take it you've heard?'

'Eppy?' Yes, everyone's heard about Eppy.'

'Can we go inside, I'd rather ask questions without having the public walking past me on the street.'

'Well, you suit yourself,' said Sarah and turned and walked away from the door. Clarissa felt it her duty to close the door behind her, despite having to scrape it across the floor. When she turned to go up the steps to the upper floor, she found she had to take them one at a time because they were so high. By the time she'd gone up, what was a dark passage, Clarissa saw at the far end of it a large wooden board and two axes sticking out of it.

'Do you always throw axes in here?' asked Clarissa.

'Don't like it out on the street,' said Sarah. Clarissa followed the sound of her voice into a small kitchen where the woman was putting the kettle on the stove.

'I believe you're Sarah Pullet, you're the cleaner at the airport. Is that correct?'

'Yes.'

'How do you find your job?' asked Clarissa. The girl looked over at her, raising her eyebrows.

'I have no idea what that's meant to mean,' said Clarissa. 'You couldn't elaborate a bit more, could you?'

'It's fine.'

Clarissa turned around in the kitchen, although there was not much space. When the kettle began to whistle, she watched the girl take a cup down, throw in a tea bag and pour a drink for herself. The cup was then taken a short distance to the table, where Sarah sat down, glaring up at Clarissa.

'Do you have a problem with the police?' asked Clarissa. 'Because you do realise this is a murder investigation and generally, most people who aren't guilty try and actually help.'

This was not strictly true. Some people just got terrified, even if they hadn't done anything wrong. Clarissa was trying to encourage the girl. In terms of being like Clarissa, the girl couldn't have been any further apart. There was a large piercing in her nose, she was dressed in black, but had a pale complexion underneath her clothes. Clarissa wore a vibrant top, her hair was a colour no natural hair ever developed, and she wore trousers that Macleod considered brash, even for a golf course.

'How long have you worked at the airport?'

'Two years.'

'Do you find it okay?'

'Yes.'

Clarissa stepped back out of the kitchen into the hall and looked at the axes driven into the wood. 'You ever mess with those things?' She turned around saw the girl shaking her head. 'What is it? Anger management therapy?'

'I just like throwing axes, nothing illegal. You can't book me for that.'

'You're right there,' said Clarissa. 'In fairness, Mr Epson wasn't hit with an axe. Speaking of Mr Epson, did you know him well?'

'Just one of them,' said the girl before picking up her tea and slurping it loudly.

'One of them? That's very awkward then, isn't it? Old style culture in a work. Do they treat you okay?'

'Who?'

'The staff there. When you're the cleaner, I get that.'

'I don't think you've ever cleaned in your life.'

'Don't you believe it,' said Clarissa. 'You've no idea what I've done, where I've been. What did they do to you, just ignore you, not talk?'

'They're all just looking down at you, aren't they? Down their noses, snobs? I'm on a cleaning job, I get basic wages, barely make the cost of living, but they're all up on the big money, aren't they? Well, the controllers, at least, and that Curtis guy, he is creepy.'

'In what way?' asked Clarissa.

'Eyeing you up, I mean, overall. It's not exactly like I'm dressed to attract and there he is standing staring at you, watching you clean. It's like some sort of a fetish or something.'

'Yes, I've met him. What about the others?'

'The controllers, I mean, you're going to interrupt them and it's, 'No, don't do that, I'm working. I'm doing this.' There isn't even a damn plane flying about. One of them actually asked me to make the tea.'

'Did you?'

'No, just half tempted to go and spit in it for him.'

'You really don't like them?'

'No, but I didn't kill anyone. I mean, I'm doing a cleaning job.' The girl stood up, took her cup back over to the kettle, filled up the same cup with the same tea bag, returned and sat down again. Clarissa wondered if this time she might get asked for a drink but was once again disappointed.

'They're not all controllers that work there, are they? What about the rest? There's a young girl working there, isn't there?'

'Yes, and she thinks she is one of them. Besides, there's only one reason she's working there.'

'Which is?' asked Clarissa.

'Curtis. He looks at me and I give him daggers. He looks at her and she's practically ready to jump into bed with him. It's pathetic.'

'You're more of a women's-lib-type person?'

'No, I'm not a women's-lib person, I just have a bit of self-respect. I don't have much; God knows I don't look like much to most people. You all call me a bit weird, a bit strange.'

'What, because you dress differently, all in black? They call me that because I dress well, with a bit more colour. I get called weird, I get called all sorts of things. I think I know where you're coming from. Tell me about the day,' said Clarissa. 'What happened?'

'Not much for me, I popped in, I think I went over to the tower about twelve. I was away by three as I was doing a little bit extra cleaning. It wasn't just the normal turnaround. I was doing a thorough clean of all the toilets. It's my big day for cleaning in there and it's only three or four hours.'

'Did you notice anything about the controllers?'

'No. Usual snobby arses but other than that, nothing.'

'When you left, did anything particular happen?'

'No. I came back here, then I went downtown. I was in a few different pubs, to be honest. I can't remember them all, woke up the next morning, and I'm here.'

'Anyone see you when you were out?' asked Clarissa.

'I wasn't out with anyone, but loads of people would have seen me, I guess, if you go and ask in the right pubs.'

'Do you want to give me the names of them?' Clarissa threw a pad down and gave the girl a pen. She wrote down three different pubs, handed them back to Clarissa.

'You can ask them. They probably know me; most people know me.'

'Okay,' said Clarissa. 'If they have seen you, then you're out of the picture. What do you think is going on? Are there any major issues in there?'

'Major issue is that airport manager, Curtis. Not just looking at the women, he's always arguing with them. He was arguing with Eppy all the time. He argued with the two girls as well and the other bloke, Harold. In fairness, Harold's not bad. He made me a cup of coffee once. It's a pity I like tea.

'Didn't he ask you?'

'Oh, I was sitting in my little den crying. I lost my mother, and he came and gave me a hug and just made sure I was okay. Then somebody said that he'd been all over me and started spreading things about him, though I told them they were wrong. That's the trouble of a place like that. It's too quiet, people want scandal, they want things to be found out. They want to just talk about this and talk about that.'

'Do you notice anything else?'

'I'm the cleaner, the stuff I notice is the fact that some of the blokes don't hit the toilet bowl. It's the fact that the cups get left on the side, sometimes. A few of the women don't know how to use the sanitary pad bin. Stuff like that.'

'Tell me about your axe-throwing.'

'I'm not allowed to tell. I just got it from a family, I throw them every now and again. Gets a little bit of anger out if you've got it.'

'Do you have a lot of anger? You feel the world has done you bad?'

'The world's done a lot of people bad and I'm all right. I try not to be snobbish like them. I try to accept everyone. I mean, I wouldn't take the mick out of you for those trousers.'

'Well, that's something because a lot of people would. Just for the record,' said Clarissa, 'confirm to me, that once you left the tower, you didn't go back?'

'I didn't go back, I got the bus to here and from here, I went out in the town. I can't get about easily; I haven't got a car. I'm on that sort of wage, just barely making things meet.'

Clarissa nodded and asked if she could go into the other room.

'Why?'

'We just like to see where everybody lives, get a picture of who they are.'

'You can look at the picture right here, nothing in the other room.'

'Well, if you don't mind then,' said Clarissa. The girl waved her arms to the air and Clarissa left the kitchen and walked into the next room along the corridor. It looked like two rooms where the dividing wall had just been dropped. At one end, was a small bed beyond which was a door, which was lying open. Inside Clarissa could see a shower and a small toilet. The rest of the large room consisted of sofa, a small TV, and a few posters, most of which have seen better days. There were a few joss sticks kicking around some candles. Clarissa turned and looked around, trying to soak up the atmosphere of the place. She saw the damp on the far wall.

'Do you pay much for this place?' asked Clarissa.

'I pay what I can afford; I can't afford much,' said Sarah, making her way into the room, still holding a cup of tea.

'Well, I don't know if I have to bother you again. I think that's all for now, but if you can think about anything, any connection between Mr Epsom and any of the rest of them, something that you think might be worth killing him for or, at least, being really angry at him for, perhaps you could give me a ring?'

Clarissa handed over her card and Sarah took it, staring at it for a moment.

'If that's what you want, then that's what I'll do, but I'm telling you what I know. It's a toxic place out there. You need to understand that. I don't see most of it, but you hear them bitching and griping at each other. If not that, then Curtis coming in there and trying to throw his weight about, that is pathetic. I don't get paid for that nonsense; that's why I don't bother with it. Do you understand that? I don't care, it's just money. It's just to help get the rest of my life running.'

'Why are you in that sort of a job? Don't you have any qualifications or anything?' asked Clarissa.

'It's honest work, I mean, it's not like I'm stealing money or anything.'

'No,' said Clarissa, 'it's just that when I talk to you, I think you're a smarter girl than what you like people to believe. You probably could have done better, but I don't know what sort of breaks you've had.'

'Your father is an alcoholic and wastes all the money, so you don't get your education properly. You don't get to go to college and then he dies, leaving bills from the people you don't want to come after you. You've just got to do what you can to pay the bills, pay them and move on with your life.'

'I guess you've got to learn to protect yourself as well,' said Clarissa.

'No,' said Sarah, 'you're reading too much into that. The axes are fun, just fun. That's all.'

Clarissa nodded and fixed her shawl around her shoulder. 'I'm sure you can get someone downstairs to do something about that door; your landlord should.'

'I don't see my landlord. You go through to the business office in town and they just don't do anything. It don't matter, anyway. This is Mull, who's going to break in? I just get on with my own little life. Nothing more, nothing less.'

Clarissa nodded. Coming back down the stairs to the front door, she noted that Sarah didn't follow her. Opening the door, Clarissa stepped out, closed it behind her, and looked up and down the street. There are probably worse places to live, but she wouldn't really want to be here either. There was a feeling about the girl, though. She was too clever for the way things were. She wasn't just a simple, pessimistic person. She understood and Clarissa got the feeling she was hiding something. She shook her head. That will be for another time, see what else everybody else has dug up, then we'll pull it all in.

Clarissa looked along the road and spotted her green sports car. She stepped inside to drive back to the airfield and rested for a moment in the car. *No*, she thought, *this wouldn't be my sort of area.*

Chapter 10

While Clarissa was in Tobermory with Sarah Pullet, Macleod had been driven to Kylie Youngs' abode, the air traffic assistant who had been in on the day of Epson's murder. In contrast to the street Clarissa had visited, Macleod was in a smart area with a block of neat flats which all had balconies giving a view out towards the harbour and its surroundings.

As Macleod approached and looked up at the recently built houses, he saw the cars parked outside in the private spaces. Most were cars he could afford but not ones he would drive around in, being slightly too flash for him. They were modern cars, not a classic like Clarissa drove. Macleod believed he was looking at people with money. Either that or they were single with no overheads.

Macleod approached the block of flats and rang a bell at the bottom. The buzzer sounded and there was a shout of, 'Who is it?'

Macleod announced himself, 'Detective Inspector Seoras Macleod,' and there was a buzz from the front door. '

'Just come,' she said quickly. Macleod stepped into the building and climbed up two flights of stairs and found Kylie

Youngs' flat.

As he approached the door, he heard a voice from inside shouting loudly, 'Come on in.' Macleod pushed open the door, closed it behind him and entered a smart living room. In the middle of the living room was an exercise bike complete with a large screen at the front of it. On top of it was a young woman pedalling hard in Lycra shorts and a crop top. Her hair was tied up behind and she glanced over at Macleod quickly.

'Just a minute, I'm working out,' she said before she went back to the screen in front of her.

Macleod looked around the flat and while it wasn't ostentatious, it did have the latest of just about everything. Clearly the woman could spend on herself. Although most of it was too gaudy for his taste, he did think she'd done it well. After a minute, Macleod noticed that she was still on the bike, but she would turn around every now and again towards him as much to see if he was looking as much as anything else.

Macleod felt uncomfortable, as the girl could have been his granddaughter. Instead, he wandered over to the window and looked at the balcony outside. It gave such a magnificent view out to the harbour.

'You must have to pay a bit for this pad,' said Macleod, trying to make conversation.

'Just a moment,' she said. 'It's the final stretch.'

Macleod turned and looked, and then looked away again quickly. She wasn't simply bent over but was now up out of the saddle. Kylie was working hard, but the angle Macleod was stood at presented the woman's buttocks moving up and down at quite a rate. Looking away, he admired the scenery, noting that the lifeboat was departing its harbour berth.

Maybe they were on exercise. He filled his mind with some

reasons that it might have been dispatched until he heard the long but deep breathing of Kylie Youngs as she stepped off the bike. He turned round and she was standing in front of him, sweating profusely.

'Sorry about that. What did you say you were? Constable someone?'

'I'm Detective Inspector Seoras Macleod. I'm investigating the murder of John Epson who I believe you worked with.'

'That's right, Eppy,' she said, wiping the sweat from her brow.

Macleod felt uncomfortable with the woman sweating and standing in such tight attire, but he tried to ignore the woman's quite deliberate attempts to get him to notice her.

'I believe you were working in the tower on the day that Mr Epson was murdered. I'd just like to ask you some questions.'

'Fire away,' said Kylie and plonked herself down on the sofa, in what Macleod thought was really not a ladylike manner. He turned his back on her.

'Mr Epson, was he popular at the airport?'

'Eppy? Oh, dear Eppy,' she said. 'Yes, I think so. Oh, he was a bit of a stickler, but I could talk to him. He liked me.' Macleod bit his lip. 'The thing is that . . . well, most people like me. That's the way I am, bright and bubbly. I seem to get on with everyone there.'

'That's great,' said Macleod, 'but I didn't ask you about you. I asked you about Mr Epson. Did he get on with everyone?'

'Oh, sometimes they had fights and spats about parts of air traffic. I don't know anything about them. It's all above my pay grade. I'm just there to book the flights in, put the strips in front of them, take the odd details and take money from aircraft that have landed, not a lot else. Curtis always said he didn't hire me for my brains.'

Macleod found this attitude difficult to comprehend. He was so used to nowadays that you had to speak to women in a certain way. One thing you certainly wouldn't have suggested was that they were employed for their looks rather than their brains. Yet here, he had a girl quite happily admitting it. With what he knew so far about Curtis James, he could believe the man would do it.

'Miss Youngs, was there anyone you particularly thought might want to do something like this to Mr Epson?'

'What? No, no way. I mean it's crazy. Isn't it? Probably some burglar or something.'

'A burglar? Stealing what?'

'Well, that's a point,' she said. 'There's the television up there, although it's not really a very good one. It's not like my one in the corner. Have you seen it? Wait till you see the colour on it!'

'Just a minute, Miss Youngs. Let's not put the TV on please; let's try and focus on the questions I'm going to ask you. You haven't been at the airport that long, have you?'

'No, a couple of years. Well, actually one.'

'You've managed to locate yourself quite well here. Haven't you?'

'Oh, yes. Yes, it pays all right. There's only me to look after though, isn't there?'

'No boyfriend or man or any woman in your life then?'

'Not at the moment, no. You don't want to get too attached too young, do you? I mean, you end up spending your money on other people then.'

'Can you just run me through what happened on the day?'

'Which day is that?' asked Kylie.

'The day that Mr Epson died. Please, if you can just

concentrate.'

'Sorry, Inspector,' she said. She stood up from the sofa and came round to in front of Macleod. Her hair was soaking wet, and her hand was now inside her crop top. Macleod found himself turning away again. Maybe he should have sent Hope to interview her, or better still, Clarissa, or maybe Ross. That would have been fun. He'd have been totally disinterested in anything she was doing.

'Look, I'm just going to go and get a shower.'

'Excuse me?' said Macleod. 'You're going to have a shower?'

'Yes,' she said. 'It won't be a problem. Look, it's just over there. I'll leave the door open. You can talk in while I'm having it.'

'I don't think that's really very appropriate.'

'Oh, you're so last century. Really? You're going to be in the door, I'm going to be in the shower. Not that you're going to see anything.'

Macleod turned to watch the woman walk to the shower. She entered the bathroom. Her top was already off and being thrown down on the floor. He turned away again. 'I need to know your movements on the day.'

'I didn't hear you, Inspector. I'm just getting everything off. That's me.'

'Are you in the shower?' asked Macleod. 'It might be wise if I just stay here until you're done.'

'No, come on over. I'm going out soon anyway. You'll have to come with me.'

'I'm not quite sure you understand how these things work.'

'I think I do, Inspector. I've watched lots on the television. They're quite good, some of them. Do you watch any of them?'

Macleod shook his head. This was not going well. He heard

the shower come on and then there was some movement and the door closing, at which time he reckoned it was probably safe to move somewhere closer to the bathroom. He walked around the rear of the sofa so he couldn't see in and stopped with his back on the wall beside the door.

'What time did you start work that morning?' he asked.

'I came in late, you see. I came in at . . . oh, hang on, dropped the soap.'

Macleod heard some fumbling about and Kylie bending down to pick it up. Then she presumably began washing again as he heard the water splash in a different fashion.

'What time did you come into work?' asked Macleod.

'I was late. I was on my own that day. I must have been what, ten? I think I worked ten to six that day, something like that. Actually, it might even have been eight to six.'

'Don't you remember?'

'No. I'm always getting things wrong. It's much easier when you're just on the normal system. You come in at the start, go home after lunch, or you come in at lunch and you go home at the end. One way or the other, it's much simpler.'

'Did Mr Epson say anything to you that day before you left?'

'Did Eppy what?'

I said, 'Did Mr Epson say anything to you that day before you left?'

'He did. Do you know what, Inspector? He did.'

'Well, what did he say?' asked Macleod, getting impatient.

'He remarked on one of the tops I was wearing. It was a new one. It was quite tight and he didn't like that. He said it should be more old-fashioned. 'Come in wearing blouse and trousers, or a skirt.' I mean, I thought it looked fine. I could show it to you later and you can tell me what you think if you like.'

89

'No,' said Macleod. 'That's not important. Did he ask or say anything to you? Something untoward, something that really struck you as strange.'

'Well, he did actually,' said Kylie. 'He said to me that he didn't understand people going on holiday for the sun. That's bizarre, isn't it?'

'I don't think so, Miss Youngs, that's not particularly weird, is it? I mean, something different. Something maybe about somebody, something maybe wasn't working right. Anything like that?'

'Oh, he had a go at Curtis.'

'The airport manager?' said Macleod, seeing the steam start to come out of the bathroom.

'Yes, Curtis, the airport manager. He came over, he was chatting to me. He does that a lot. Anyway, he came over and . . . oh, hang on a minute; that's me done. Just a second. I'll be out.' Macleod looked away from the door. Heard the girl get out. Then a towel starting to be used.

'What did he say to you, Miss Youngs?

'Well, there's . . . hey, I'll come out.' Macleod got no warning as the girl stepped out of the shower room. He thanked his God that she'd actually put on a dressing gown, although, in his mind, it was a poor excuse for one.

'He said to me that he liked what I was wearing. I remember because Eppy said to him, "You shouldn't be encouraging the girl." But I don't understand what he meant by that. Curtis said, "There's nothing wrong with a good-looking young lady." I thought that was quite nice.'

Macleod walked over to the window again, putting some distance between himself and Kylie Youngs. 'I suggest, Miss Youngs, that you go and get changed. We'll continue our conversation afterwards. I don't really think it's appropriate for me to interview in your current state of dress.'

'All right. Well, if that's how you feel, I was just trying to save you a bit of time. I'll just go through to the bedroom then.'

Macleod heard her footsteps moving away to the bedroom. Then he turned around and started looking around the room, which seemed to contain an awful lot of photographs. In all of them the central person was Kylie. There were a lot of photographs with just her. He found this a bit bizarre. People living on their own weren't prone to putting lots of photographs of themselves up. It'd be family members, or maybe friends but not usually themselves. Kylie seemed to be the main feature in all the photographs. There were also a number of men in each.

He was quite surprised at the number where it was just her and a group of men. Maybe she was of that ilk; she just liked the male company. In truth, it was bugging him. He felt uncomfortable, almost cursing himself that he hadn't told Hope to come and do this. As he was shaking his head, he spotted a number of photographs that seemed to have Eppy in them and a number of the other male airport employees. Curtis was there too. There were no female controllers with them though. Maybe they were just out of shot but it seemed that Kylie always had to be surrounded by men.

As he picked one up to look at it, he heard her walk out of the bedroom and come back into the living room. He looked up and almost thought that what she was wearing on the bike was more appropriate to go out in than what she had on now.

'I'm just going to get a little bite, Inspector. If you want to come with me, you can. I don't like to overdress for going out.'

Macleod tried to keep an impassive face, but he also saw her looking very closely at a photograph he had picked up in his hand. Kylie came over, took it off him, and looked at it closely.

'Yes, that's Eppy with me. That's the work's night out. They are good guys, they are. Great fun to be about. I think they liked me amongst their company, a bit of glamour. Curtis's always over and pulling at me. He said to me . . . did I tell you? He hired me for my looks, not for my brains.'

'You did say,' said Macleod. 'Why don't you get a coat, and we'll go and get something to eat, then we can discuss things further.'

'Oh, I don't need a coat. I mean, it's not exactly cold out there.' Macleod looked at her. He swore he would feel cold in Spain wearing what she was wearing.

Chapter 11

Macleod felt his phone vibrate as he descended the steps from Kylie Youngs' flat. He picked up the call and didn't recognise the number but answered it anyway.

'Detective Inspector Seoras Macleod.'

'This is Curtis James. Macleod, you need to open my airport. I'm haemorrhaging money hand over fist here. Your people should be done by now.'

Macleod stopped in his tracks, almost taken aback by the man's tone.

'I'm afraid that's not how it works, Mr James.'

'Call me Curtis.'

'No, Mr James. The way it works is I come in to do an investigation. While I need places to be shut for that, they are shut until I deem that I have conducted my studies and I'm happy with them. At that point, I hand the areas back to those who wish to do something with them. At the moment, your airport is shut because we are working there. You have had a murder committed on your premises, and frankly, I'm a bit cheesed off that you seem more concerned about putting the airport back into commission than about dealing with the fact you have a murderer in your midst.'

'Now, look here, Seoras.'

Did he just call me Seoras? thought Macleod. *He didn't seriously just call me Seoras.*

'The name is Detective Inspector Macleod. That is the only name you get to call me. You can use Inspector for short if you really wish, Mr James. At the moment, I'm in the middle of conducting an investigation, and I'd like it if you would hang up immediately.'

'Now look here, Macleod, that's just not good enough. I'm going to be getting our Councillor on to you.'

'You can get the Councillor, your MP, the Prime Minister and whoever else you want on to me. I am in the middle of an investigation. Now, if you want to discuss this further, I'll give you a number to call.' Macleod rhymed off a number. 'Have you got that one, Mr James?'

'I have, Macleod. Who's this person I'll speaking to?'

'That'll be somebody who can deal with the business. I think you'll find them very firm, but fair. Don't forget to tell them that Detective Inspector Macleod sent you.'

'Oh, I'll do that, Macleod. Don't you worry,' said Curtis James. 'Frankly, it's a disgrace. If all policemen worked like you, nothing would get done.'

'Just you call that number, Mr James. Remember to tell them that I sent you, that I gave you every assistance. In fact, tell them, both barrels.'

The line was closed. Macleod put his mobile away into his pocket and turned back to Kylie, who he still felt should be dressed in a jacket, at least.

'There's a nip in the air out here,' he said and watched as she giggled at him.

'You're very funny in some ways, aren't you, Inspector? Sorry, I don't mean that to be rude, but you really are. What would you like to eat?'

'I just want a bite,' said Macleod. 'Just take me somewhere here that's good.'

'Just follow me then.'

As Kylie descended the last of the stairs, Macleod followed and then felt his phone vibrating again. He picked it up, ready to see if it was Curtis James, but instead, he saw Ross's image on the screen.

'Yes, Macleod.'

'Sorry to bother you, sir. It's just that Clarissa said to me that she's got Curtis James on the phone to her. He's claiming that you sent him to her so she could sort out opening the airfield.'

'I sent him to her to talk about why we can't open the airfield and also, with a message that she was to give him every assistance with both barrels.'

Macleod could hear Ross almost swallow hard and then there was a slight chortle. 'Something wrong, Ross?'

'No, nothing. I think that the sergeant was just wanting to check that that was the correct message.'

'You make sure you tell her.'

'She's just heard, Inspector, and I can tell you right now, that both barrels are being emptied.' Macleod thought he could hear Clarissa's voice in the background.

'When she comes off the phone, Ross, just tell her thanks from me. If he gives us any more hassle, tell Clarissa she can just go at him all she wants, bring Hope in if she wants to really annoy him.'

'Will do,' said Ross, almost laughing. 'Do you need a car soon?'

'I'm just down in Tobermory. I'll probably be another hour, then send someone down to pick me up.'

'Very good, sir. Will do that.'

Macleod turned back to Kylie Youngs and apologised before following her into town. As they walked along the streets, he could see certain men looking at her, but instead of shying away, she literally turned around and almost waved hello at them. Macleod felt she was quite brazen, but today was a different day and certainly not how he was brought up. He'd been told several times by Jane to stop being an old stick in the mud, just to let people be people. Well, that was all right, but if this was his daughter, he'd be having a word.

Kylie led them through to a cafe along the front of the bay where they took seats inside. Macleod could see her yet again, looking around, almost trying to find any man to smile at.

'If you don't mind me asking, Miss Youngs?'

'Would you call me Kylie? Nobody calls me Miss Youngs. It sounds like I'm in court.'

'Indeed, but I am being formal here,' said Macleod. 'Miss Youngs, you seem to quite like male attention. I don't mean in a small way. You seem to actively go out and seek it.'

'Well, yes. Nothing wrong with that, is there, Inspector?'

'Well, there's certainly nothing illegal about it,' said Macleod, and then realised how bad a statement he just made.

'I appreciate it may not have been done in your day, but nowadays, some of us girls go after the men. We're allowed to, you know that. It's quite a turn-on when you see them staring at you.'

'Right,' said Macleod. 'It's just I was wondering, were you that way with any of the male controllers or for that matter, the female ones? I'm not aware of where you sit on that particular fence.'

Macleod almost hung his head at making a hash of a second question.

'Oh, it's all right, Inspector. No, I'm purely orientated towards the men, but I haven't been in any relations with the male controllers. John Epson, come on. As nice a guy as he was and he was nice, he wouldn't have done anything like that. He was straight-laced, even more so than yourself. Harold would have been nice, though. Seven kids. He treats people well. Yes, he certainly would have interested me, but he never showed any interest. I always felt like he was my dad or something, the way he spoke to me at times. Pleasant though.'

'You had no relations with anyone up at the airport?'

'Oh, yes, I have,' said Kylie. 'Curtis, I mean, it was with Curtis.'

Macleod nearly spat out his coffee. 'Really?' he said. 'That's the sort of guy you would go for?'

'No, not go for. No, no, I needed to get the job when I went to the interview there, so I propositioned him. I'd seen him at the airport before, you can tell when a guy is casting the eye and frankly, he was casting like he had a trawler's net. It didn't take much, a couple of suggestions, back in the interview room, I already had the answers to any other questions.'

Macleod's face became contorted.

'With all due respect, Miss Youngs, there's one thing to seek to get men's attention and then to engage in a relationship with him or even a single night's stand, but you're using it to coerce, to use your body as a payment. I'm not sure how ethical that is, even if this is the modern age.'

'Well, if that's the way you see it, fair enough. It's okay. I was just a young girl getting ahead. Some people have brains, I don't, but I do have a figure and it gets me places that my brains never would.'

'Has he ever sought for more payment, so to speak?'

'Has he ever asked for more sex?' said Kylie. 'No, he hasn't. He comes over and he intimates this and that, but he's never followed through on anything.'

'I find that quite strange. Do you have some other sort of hold over him?' asked Macleod.

'It's not that, it's just that when we, well, did the deed for the job, he was not impressive. I think he was a bit embarrassed. I also think he was a bit scared, that if he didn't give me the job, I was going to go and tell some people.'

Inside, Macleod felt thoroughly disgusted, even if he thought the man was getting his comeuppance.

'You've got to see it from my point of view, Inspector. What would I be doing? I'd probably be like that Sarah, cleaning toilets all day long, looked down upon by everyone else and then I'd end up shacked up with some drunken guy who'd beat me about, all the best years of my youth gone to waste. I know you may not agree with this, but this was my route to find an independent life. I wasn't going to go down that road of just being some scrubber.'

Macleod thought of how that word, in the past, would probably describe exactly, how people of that time would have thought of Kylie today, but he let the thought pass.

'Did anybody ever know about this, the fact that you and Curtis James had had sex in order for you to get the job?'

'Well, I didn't tell anybody directly, of course not. If I admitted to it, other people could have come back and had a go about the interview process.'

'You just admitted it to me, though,' said Macleod.

'Yes, I have, Inspector, but I've done it because you're

investigating a murder. It's quite horrific what happened and while you may look at me and think, "Oh, she's just some big flirt or she's a dumb blonde," I'm not dumb. You need to make sure that I'm not involved, so I'm going to be as clean as I can with you, and I hope you appreciate that.

Kylie leaned forward and Macleod found himself having to look out the window.

'I do appreciate your candour, Miss Youngs, though I can't say that I approve of your lifestyle or the actions you've taken. Maybe that's just because I'm an old fart or maybe it's because my standards are correct; other people can judge that. As regards to the murder investigation, I thank you for being so forward. It's much appreciated.'

Macleod looked down and he picked up the prawn sandwich that was on a plate in front of him. He bit into it and it tasted rather good. After he'd swallowed, he took a drink of his coffee, and looked back across the table.

'You also picked a rather good spot to eat and considering how famished my stomach was, I thank you for that as well.'

'Very kind of you to say so, Inspector. I think we understand each other, don't we? I'm not asking for your approval, and you certainly wouldn't give it, and you certainly wouldn't look for my approval on what you do. But I am being honest and genuine.'

'I think you are,' said Macleod, and resumed eating his lunch. When he left the building, he pondered at his attitude. Kylie Youngs may be honest despite how much he detested the way she went about things with men. As he walked along the front of Tobermory, he thought about making a phone call to Ross, to get him a squad car. His phone rang instead.

'Seoras, It's Clarissa. You need to come quick; I've got Ross sending you a car.'

'Why, what's up?'

'It's Sara Pullet, sir. She's been found dead in her home.'

'Found dead?'

'It appears so. Some sort of an attack.'

'How did we find out?'

'A phone call from Curtis James. Direct to me, not a niner. Seems he was the one who found her.'

Chapter 12

Macleod stepped out of the police squad car and approached a broken door. The battered fixture had a hinge off at the bottom and the top one looked like it was barely hanging on. The rest of the lock on the right-hand side was bent away but Macleod reckoned the door must have been forced. He was standing outside, not prepared to go in until Hope came down the stairs and appeared at the front door dressed in a white overall.

'There's a set of coveralls in the boot of the car, just outside,' said Hope, pressing the button on her keys. 'You better get the stuff on. Jona's not here yet. She's on her way.'

'Oh, she'll have our guts for garters if I walk in uncovered.' Macleod strode to the back of Hope's car, put on his white coverall and hood and then stepped inside Sarah Pullet's house.

'She's up the top, sir,' said Hope, coming up behind him. 'Take a right then straight on towards the living room.' As Macleod reached the top of the stairs and turned round in the small hallway, he saw a board with a couple of axes in it.

'These got anything to do with it?'

'We don't think so. Just keep going, Seoras. I'll show you where it is.'

Macleod walked along the corridor and then turned off into a living room. Over at the bed, he saw a body lying across it, the sheets soaked in blood. He stepped across, got as close as he could without stepping in the puddle of red, and looked towards the throat.

'It looks cut,' he said. 'Similar to Mr Epson. Any weapons around?'

'Other than the axes, not really. Checked the kitchen for knives, but everything's clean in there. Best to leave it to Jona to work out if any of those were part of it. We also found Sara's mobile, but I'll get it to Ross once Jona's checked it over. We'll see if there were any recent calls.'

'If they came in here to do this, they might be lucky enough and could have got behind her and therefore not got covered in the blood. Although, they'd have to be a pretty smart operator, but they'd then have the knife. Maybe you stick it in your coat, go and get rid of it. Get a search going on Hope, out and down along the shore and around Tobermory. Also, all the roads and hedges you can dump into, but the sea's probably a good bet down by the rocks. Last time our killer didn't go too far before dumping. We also haven't told anybody that we found it.'

'Well, Curtis James knows we've found it. You think he's going to keep quiet?'

'I don't know what to think regards Mr James, but whatever, I don't think it's general knowledge yet. None of the suspects I've talked to have mentioned it.'

'Okay, I'll get on it. Probably going to need to call in other agencies as well. We don't have a lot of people, same as we did at the airport.'

'Go to it,' said Macleod. As he turned around, he saw Clarissa approaching, also dressed up in a white coverall but which was decidedly struggling against what presumably was her shawl underneath.

'Where's Curtis James then?' said Macleod.

'He's in the kitchen and he's not in a good way. I just thought I'd pop in and tell you.'

'Well, let's go see him.' Macleod entered the kitchen and found it was a tight squeeze for the three of them to be inside. Curtis James was sitting on a seat, a cup of tea in front of him but was shaking immensely.

'What were you doing here, Mr James?'

'Did you see it?' he said. 'It's the blood everywhere. Every where's blood. Why? I mean, Sarah, she was lovely. Strange, different, but lovely in her own way. I don't understand it. I don't. I don't.'

'Why were you here, Mr James?' asked Macleod.

'I just popped in to if see she was all right. Just checking up on my staff.'

'What was the real reason you were here?' asked Clarissa.

'I just told you.'

'No, Mr James. What was the real reason you were here? When I interviewed Sarah earlier on, she said that you always had an eye for her. To be frank, you seem to have an eye for most women. Were you hoping to come around and, what, cuddle her better, have a chat about Mr Epson and see if she broke down a little, needed a shoulder to cry on?'

The man stared at Clarissa. 'Is that what you take me for?'

'Frankly,' said Macleod, 'yes, and I think my sergeant's correct even if she's being very direct about it.'

'You people are all the same. Thinking the worst motives of everyone.'

'Then why were you here?' asked Clarissa. 'Sarah didn't like you. You weren't best pals with her. As far as she was concerned, your lot never paid her any attention. Well, except you did but only in lecherous tones.'

'How dare you?'

'Oh, I dare,' said Clarissa. 'We've got two dead people and I dare.'

'The sergeant's correct. What were you doing here? Did you have any relations with her?'

'Relations? What do you mean relations?'

'He means sex. It's the polite word we use,' said Clarissa.

'I'm not a man who goes around having sex with younger women.'

'Strangely enough, Mr James, I know that not to be correct,' said Macleod and took a glance from Clarissa. 'In fact, I heard that you're quite happy to have sex with young women if they wish to acquire certain jobs. Did Sarah acquire her job in that fashion?'

'She did not.'

'I'm not sure she did, boss,' said Clarissa.

'No, but somebody did, and I think that's why our friend here was round. We'll search the place for fingerprints. We'll see if he forced the door.'

'I didn't. That's why I came in. Don't you understand? The door was broken. I came in to check she was all right and when I did, she was . . . oh God, she was covered in blood. There was just blood everywhere, up and down.'

'Did you clock a knife anywhere?' asked Clarissa.

'A what?'

'A knife. Her throat was slit. We're trying to find the knife. Did you clock a knife anywhere?'

'No, I didn't. How could I clock a knife?' Then Curtis James suddenly became much more controlled. 'And I've something else to tell you. That if any of these people say I've had sex with them, it's a lie. I'm not that sort of person. I'm a married man. I have a wife. You know? And tell me, when can I open my airport?'

'I told you before, Mr James,' said Macleod. 'You'll have to speak to Sergeant Urquhart here about that, but it won't be today.' Macleod turned to Clarissa. 'Let's get everybody out of here, go down and talk to Jona when she arrives.'

'Your ever-reliable forensic officer is here,' said a diminutive Asian woman stepping into the kitchen, 'but we'll not talk about that in here as this seems to be quite small. Can I see you in the next room, Inspector?'

'Of course, Miss Nakamura. Sergeant, deal with Mr James.' Macleod followed Jona through to the living room where the two of them stood looking at the body.

'I've had a brief investigation. Yes, her throat's slit quite severely. As you can see, there's a lot of blood. Looking quickly around the knives that are in the room, the murder weapon is not here. The blades, they aren't deep enough. I'm looking for quite a big blade.'

'What about the axes?'

'Too thick,' said Jona, 'way too thick. I saw Sergeant McGrath outside setting up teams to search. I suggest that you let my team get on in here, Inspector, and you base yourself outside. Commandeer somewhere and I'll set up a cordon around the area and we'll get to work. See if we can tidy this place up by the end of tomorrow.'

'Of course,' said Macleod. 'Just keep me appraised of anything.'

* * *

At five in the morning, Hope McGrath was feeling jaded. Another coffee had arrived but quite frankly, she wasn't sure she could drink any more. It wasn't the tastiest coffee to begin with, and she was so tired that all she wanted to do was collapse into bed. Macleod had gone off for a sleep because she had told him to. After all, everything was in motion. All they could do was look for the weapon. Coastguard teams were out, local fire crew as well, even some volunteers who had search and rescue experience.

They'd started along the shore, several of the police teams working further inland making their way back and forward, but so far, they'd found nothing. Hope had the experts work out from Sarah Pullet's flat, and by now they were well beyond the radius that it had taken the first killer to drop the knife into the car in the fire ground. Hope wondered if soon they should double back because the thing about killers was, they were fairly repetitive, especially when they knew a system worked.

The radio attached to Hope's side crackled into life, and she heard the search advisor talking to one of the search parties giving details of a find. She picked up the radio and advised she was on the way and for no one to touch it. Ross was also on scene and together they travelled in the car down to the coast, less than a kilometre away where they saw a number of people standing around with torches on their heads, pointing down to the ground amongst the rocks.

'It's down there,' said a man dressed in blue. Hope produced her torch, got down on her front and peered down into a gap between three rocks. With the torch out in front of her, she could see the edge of a blade. The blade was long but flat, quite

106

wide, or at least what Hope could see of it.

'Do you want me to bring it up?' asked the man.

'No,' said Hope. 'We don't touch it. The forensic team will be over. They might require your assistance to get it out, but they'll tell you how to do it. We don't want to disturb any of the prints or potential contaminating marks on the knife.' As Hope stood up, she felt a few spits of rain and looked out to the sea, which was only three or four metres away.

'Is that tide coming in?' she asked the man in blue.

'It is, indeed. They'll need to be down here in the next hour or two to get the knife. We've been quite lucky. It seems that the tide must have been going the wrong way for the killer,' he said. 'I suspect they were looking to dump it in so it could flush away with the sea. Looks like the tide had already missed it.'

Hope picked up her phone and called Jona Nakamura.

'Well, what a lovely time of the morning to speak to you,' she said. 'Tell me you got something for me, that it's not just a pleasant call or my order for a croissant.'

'Jona,' said Hope, 'found a knife. I think it's the one. Take the road down out towards the coast and you'll see us. Load of wagons with flashing lights on top, can't miss us. You tell your guys to pick the knife out, though as it's trapped down between two rocks. You've got an hour or two before the tide comes and washes over it.'

'On my way now,' she said. It took Jona about ten minutes to arrive, and then she sprinted over in her white suit, ushering everyone else back. She reached down into the gap and realised that she was too small to go the full distance down. Jona turned around and shouted at a few of the men to grab her feet. Hope watched as the Asian woman was lowered into the gap and then came back up with a knife clutched in her gloved hands. Carefully, she turned to one of her assistants who'd opened a bag for her to drop it into.

'Don't want to be rude, everyone, but we probably should look through this area as well. However, having stood all over it, we may not get a chance.'

'But we had to be looking for the knife. You can't tippy-toe everywhere,' said one guy.

'Not having a go,' said Jona. 'Just explaining to the sergeant that we might not find anything. Thank you for your efforts, though. Could be crucial finding the knife.'

The man smiled over at Jona. 'Sorry,' he said, 'just been a long night.'

'For us all,' she said. 'This knife looks the same,' she said to Hope, 'as the one at the airport, so I think we've found it. You can probably stand these people down if you're happy.'

Hope nodded, turned around, and dismissed the search advisor, thanking all the team. She said she'd meet back up with them at the search start so they could have a short debrief about what had happened. It was still spitting rain and she decided she'd need to get inside soon.

'You got enough people coming down to help here?' asked Hope.

'Just leave it to me,' said Jona. 'You always ask, but I've done this so often I can do it in my sleep.'

Ross was sitting on a rock over from Hope, and she turned to ask him to make his way back with her. He held up a phone inside a plastic bag.

'Sergeant,' he said, 'I've managed to get into it. It's funny how many people just have a nominal code, 0000 or 1111. It makes getting into the phones quite easy.'

'You find anything good?' asked Hope.

'Not a lot, except for this. The last number on the phone is an international number. Bit unusual. I need to get back and trace it, though, see if it comes up with something good.'

'Well, you best get on it soon. It's after, what, half five now. Boss will be here anytime and we'd better have something for him.'

Chapter 13

Macleod's arrival in the morning led to his team suddenly feeling rejuvenated as their boss toured around the different scenes, thanking and encouraging those who had worked through the night. He decided to call a conference for ten o'clock, pulling everyone in together and was generously offered the lifeboat station down by the harbour. On his arrival, the launch operations manager had prepared coffee and even organised some croissants for breakfast. Macleod thanked him gratefully as his team settled into the room. Most had been up through the night. Macleod was just keen to bring everything together and understand what was going on.

'First up, everyone, thank you for your effort so far. It seems that our killer has struck again, and we'll try and compare the two crimes and see if there's any discrepancies between them. However, at this point, I think we may be looking for the same suspect. The first person I'm going to bring in is Jona Nakamura, our chief forensic officer, who's going to give us as much background as she can from what forensics have found so far.'

Jona stepped forward and Macleod could see the bags under

her eyes, but as ever, the woman was professional and had set up a small display using a projector that ran off her laptop. On the white wall behind her appeared a picture of a knife.

'As we know, both our victims had their throats cut by a knife. What is quite unusual, if you look at the picture behind me, is that we've actually got a circus knife. On both occasions, it was a circus knife, but both had one side sharpened. Normally, these things are fairly blunt because when you're throwing it at a body going round and round, the last thing you need put is to actually penetrate the skin if you make a mistake. You might get a bit of bruising, it might bounce off, but what you want it to do is sink in with an impact on the large screen behind the supposed victim. However, these particular knives have been sharpened so that if you cut with the edge, it will cut deep. Normally, you would just bruise into the neck. That's the first thing,' she said.

'The second thing is that, yes, they are a match; they're large throwing knives. They're from a circus background, which could be important. Why would somebody kill with one of these? I wouldn't. I'd just get a kitchen knife and hack the neck apart. These are not weapons of chance; these are weapons for a reason. There is a statement being made here for one reason or another.

'Sarah Pullet was surprised from behind at her bed and then cut open so the blood copiously poured out around the room. The knife was then taken and deposited out towards the coast in between some rocks. Now again, it seems that we were lucky in the sense that the tide was on its way out. What bothers me is why would someone look to dispose of this knife?'

'What are you saying?' asked Macleod.

'I think what Jona's meaning,' said Hope, 'is why would you

111

make a statement with a knife like this? Sharpening the blade, using it, even though it's the worst thing you can use, and then try to get rid of it? You want to leave it. You want it to be found.'

'She's right, Inspector. I think we were meant to find this. I think they understood what the tide was doing. I'm assuming as well, what with the first knife going into the car on the fire practice ground, we were meant to find these knives. They're meant to say something. They're meant to give a reason for the killing. Whether that reason is from someone who's doing the killing or whether it's meant to frame someone, I don't know.'

'Did you find anything else out about Sarah Pullet, though?' asked Macleod.

'Quite a bit, actually, Inspector. Sarah Pullet was a drug user. When I examined her body, I could see where she'd used needles before, but she very much held it together from what we can gather. According to Sergeant McGrath and Sergeant Urquhart, it seems that Sarah had a dark persona, which covered up a lot of her opposite-mindedness or shakiness, things where you would say that person doesn't look right. You don't say so, or rather you attribute it slightly differently, when that person is meant to be weird in her own right.

'What you're saying,' said Macleod 'is that Sarah wasn't really this dark persona. She played it as cover.'

'Not uncommon though, is it?' said Ross. 'With some drug addicts, some people look fine because that's the way they are. They're able to have this bigger persona that's bigger than the drugs and what it does to them.'

'But there were drugs found in her house?' asked Macleod.

'Very much so,' said Clarissa. 'I spoke to the local police

force and they said they're having a problem with drugs on the island at the moment. The biggest problem they have is they don't understand how they're getting in. They've targeted the ferry, actually had the dogs over to sniff out. They've tried the passenger flights coming in.'

'Do they get any other sort of flights in?'

'They do get local flights, but again, they've done random checks on some of those and they've not come through. It doesn't appear that the drugs are coming in either on the ferry or on flights.'

'Could they be coming through anywhere else? I mean, does Sarah have any other people she saw regularly?' asked Macleod.

'Nothing from her house at the moment. I've tried the neighbours; it seems like the girl barely went out at all,' said Clarissa. 'When I spoke to her, she was good. I wouldn't have guessed she was on drugs. I'd have said she was a sharp individual. I don't know how much of a user she was. She's not a typical junkie.'

'You think she, what, just used recreationally? Could have been involved in some other side of it?' asked Ross.

'It's a possibility,' said Clarissa. 'I don't have that much experience in these sorts of things, but I would say maybe.'

'What about her phone?' asked Macleod. 'You said she contacted an international number last. Where are we with that?'

'Well, I rang it and it connected in Iceland, but then hung up,' said Ross. 'When I then contacted again, discovered it's an Icelandic pay-as-you-go number. It seems like the SIM card's no longer working.'

'Well, that is interesting,' said Macleod, 'but that'll be a dead end now. Still, it's how traffickers work at times. Isn't it? Working on the pay-as-you-go numbers, using them once.'

'I think she was heavily involved,' said Hope. 'Jona found a selection of numbers on different pieces of paper within the house. Looks like those are our numbers to call.'

'Have we tried calling any more of them?' asked Macleod.

'Been on it for the last hour,' said Clarissa, 'along with Ross. Every time you ring them, they're just dead. They're gone. I spoke again to the telecommunications company and it seems like those SIM cards aren't active. Can't trace them. Can't do anything like that. I feel that looks like a dead-end in terms of investigation but maybe it does give a reason for why she was killed. Drugs.'

'It's not sitting well with Mr Epson, is it?' said Macleod. 'There's no indications he was a drug user nor a drug patient. In fact, the way he was, his nature, would suggest he would be against it.'

'Maybe he was a victim because he stood up against it,' said Clarissa. 'Maybe that could be it.'

'That's if it is drugs,' said Ross. 'Doesn't necessarily mean it was. We're saying drugs because one of our victims is involved in them. It could be a different reason, but she just happens to be a drug partaker.'

Macleod stood up and began to walk around the room. He looked over and saw Clarissa munching on a croissant and she almost apologetically put it down, but Macleod waved his hand indicating she could continue. 'If you're all hungry, just eat,' he said. 'Just stay focused. What else are you going to do, Miss Nakamura?' he asked.

'I've still got a bit more work to do, trying to see if I can get a hit for our killer. I need more details about them, and see if we can pick up any DNA.'

'How long are we going to be on the airfield for?'

'Should be clear soon. I doubt we'll need to keep it locked down for much longer.'

'Fine,' said Macleod and turned to Clarissa. 'Curtis James,' he said. 'What do you make of him? What do you think he was doing there with Sarah Pullet?'

'Well, he could just be a lech and trying to get in with her. Not quite sure how far he'd go with that. When I spoke to her, she said she could handle him. She was well aware that he was looking at her but didn't complain about any actions he was taking.'

'It's the same problem again, isn't it?' said Hope. 'You're looking at the killer for two people saying one's a lech in targeting women and yet the first person to die was a man.'

'Who may again have objected to people's behaviour,' said Macleod. 'Everything's just too tenuous. The only thing we've got is the circus knife. They seem to be quite poignant in what's happening.'

'I would caution against it,' said Jona. 'Be very open-eyed about it. Like I said, it seems to me we were meant to find these. They weren't hidden away well. This is not how I would dispose of a knife if I killed someone.'

'But you also know too much,' said Macleod, and received a glare from Jona. 'But your point is taken. Okay, Jona, you keep on it. Let me know when you're finished at the airport or at the house. Clarissa, get into the airfield with Ross. I want to know who's coming in and going out. This looks like it could be a drug killing, in which case, we need to find that angle. Talk to the local branch here, find out who they've checked. Go over their work. Make sure it's solid. Give them a hand if you need to. The other person we haven't spoken to is Julia Fluke, the other trafficker. We were going to go round there until this kicked off, so I'll make sure I see her today. One of the problems we've got is anybody could have come in. Ross, did you check any CCTV on the street?'

'None for the door. I've looked around for any I can get, but there's not a lot. It's not the crime capital of the world here, not like the centre of Inverness or Glasgow. CCTV is few and far between. I already checked and I can't see anything untoward or anybody we already know who shouldn't be in the picture.'

'The other thing, Clarissa, is Curtis James—get on to him. Not him personally but actually get into his backstory, his life. See what you can dig up about him. Hope, oversee that. Keep on top of everything as usual and you can come along with me to Julia Fluke so we have a chat with her.

'I know you've all been up and I may ask you to continue, but if you can, find an hour or two for sleep. Hopefully, tonight will be a normal night. You can all crash at the hotel. They've got a good breakfast, haven't they? Now, let's go.'

Macleod took his cup of coffee on his way out of the room. Walking out to the harbour side, he stood looking out over the bay at Tobermory. He was joined from behind by Hope McGrath.

'You're okay, Seoras?' she asked.

'Gosh, just that time, isn't it? Usual thing, so many leads. Which one do you pull on? Pull on the wrong one, somebody can die if you don't get the right one quick enough. Usual story.'

'Something's bugging you though as well, isn't it?'

'Curtis James,' said Macleod. 'I don't trust him. He comes on and all about the airport, this and that. I just sometimes

116

wonder, is it a diversion tactic? That's why I want Clarissa to look deeper and find out what's happening.'

'The problem with him is that he seems to be too good a suspect. You don't like him. I don't like him. Heck, I walked past him the other day and he checked out my backside for nearly ten seconds. And then when he gets caught, he does this sort of giggle; it's almost like—I don't know.'

'Exactly,' said Macleod,' because I really want to take him down. It's like you want to put him away and everything starts to point vaguely in that direction and then you just go, 'Oh, it must be.' We need to be careful, Hope. The circus knife. What Jona said was right. Is somebody messing with us? Is somebody setting up a victim? And if they are, we need to be smart enough to clear that name and get the right one.'

Macleod looked out on to the morning water and saw the sun reflecting off of it. The day was cold, but the skies were clear, and inside he still had a little bit of trepidation, the type he always seemed to have around any case. He lifted his cup and drained it and then turned to Hope.

'Time to go to work. It's a beautiful day for it.'

Chapter 14

Clarissa rummaged through the printouts in front of her, crossing off all the routine traffic and local flights that were coming through the airport. Macleod had tasked her to find out if any drugs were coming in that way, and also to check through whether the local police had missed anything. She was looking for patterns, anything on a regular basis coming through. As she examined the documents, she realised that there didn't seem to be any flights coming from outside the United Kingdom. She placed a call to Harold Lyme, who Macleod had said seemed to be on top of his game with regards to being an air traffic controller.

'Mr Lyme, it's Detective Sergeant Clarissa Urquhart with the investigation team. I was just wondering if you could help me. I'm looking at flights arriving at the airport. Every flight seems to be coming from within the UK. Is that normal?'

'Well, it is because we're not one of the entry ports for other flights coming in. To be honest, on the commercial side of it, no one's coming direct from another country. We're too small an airport really for that. On the other side of it, ferry flights—that's people who are bringing aircraft across the Atlantic or out of Europe to go across to America—they don't tend to stop with us. They have to be further north, maybe Stornoway, Shetland, up that way. You have to be a registered port to fly into in the first place, and we're not.'

'So, everyone that's coming to you is basically a UK citizen?' asked Clarissa.

'No, that wouldn't be the case. We get some foreign pilots coming through, people on tours, flying here, there, wherever. If you get an irregular flight coming in from abroad, we have to hold the aircraft. We have to talk to customs about it because normally, they wouldn't fly into here.'

'Do you get many of those?'

'No, it's much easier for them to fly in further north.'

'Do you get anyone coming from overseas, then coming from another airport down to here? For instance, would somebody fly into Stornoway and then fly down to yourselves in Mull?'

'It's not really far enough for a lot of them to do that, what with their flight time, better to land further on down. Ferry pilots, their job is basically to take a plane from here to there. They're not into sightseeing on the way. Get up in the air, get the aircraft to wherever it needs to be, pick up your money, go home.'

'Do the planes get searched on arrival?'

'No, not for coming to the private aprons. Now, if you're up on the main apron and they're a scheduled flight, security has to check everybody on; it's what's called a critical area, or it's like a control zone. So, you know that that aircraft has taken off from within a controlled zone at one airport, landed, and gone into the other one. So, it's not been touched in between. If they're going down to someone on the smaller airplane, well, it could have come from anywhere. People can come up to the small apron. We don't encourage people to run around airside,

119

but if someone was to ask to go in, there's nothing really to stop them if they know the pilot or anyone who's landed, as long as someone lets them through the gate.'

'I see,' said Clarissa. 'Just for instance, if you were running drugs and you popped them in an aircraft, you can land in that lower apron and come off again and security would never check.'

'That's correct. They're not there to check. Security checks the scheduled aircraft, the commercial ones that are running up on the main apron.'

'Did you ever see the police down with the dogs checking the small aircraft that came in?'

'Rarely. Not that often at all, to be truthful. There's not that many have come through on a routine basis. In the summer, you get people fly in and go around Mull for a bit, but you're not talking about people coming back and forward, back and forward all the time. To be honest, I don't think there's that many coming on a routine basis that would allow for it, or you could check back.'

'There's definitely no one coming from Iceland?' asked Clarissa, thinking about the phone numbers that have been traced from Sarah Pullet's flat.

'That's correct. Well, I say that's correct, but I wouldn't know. As a controller sat up there, all you see is where they took off from. If they took off from Stornoway, you'd see it. If they took off from Shetland, East Midlands, anywhere in the UK, that's what you'd see. If they took off from Reykjavík, it would be on the strip. I've never seen Reykjavík on the strip.'

'The strip?' asked Clarissa.

'Sorry,' said Harold, 'force of habit. We have strips in front of us with details of each of the aircraft we're working. On it, it will say on the arrival strip where that aircraft came from. When they're departing, it tells us where they're going to. It's a legal requirement you have to advise the air traffic unit at the very least of that. Or you might have to file a flight plan depending on certain conditions.'

'I'm having a look at the day of Mr Epson's death. It said that there's a flight that came down from the north. Seemed to have come from Stornoway. Is that correct?'

'I think there was one that day. I mean, I couldn't honestly tell you. What does it say on the strip?'

'I don't have that. I just have the details afterwards put on a piece of paper. It says it came down from Stornoway, then headed off to Blackpool.'

'All right. Yes. I think I departed that one. Twin engine, ferry flight. I think that's a one-off. Didn't recognise the aircraft.'

'Did you recognise the pilot at all?'

'Well, he didn't come into the VCR, the visual control room where we work from. If he doesn't do that, I won't.'

'You said it was a ferry flight; is that correct?'

'Yes,' said Harold, 'a ferry flight. You only ever see those aircraft once.'

'Well, thank you for your time,' said Clarissa.

Clarissa walked to an office Macleod was occupying and filled him in with the details. Jona had cleared up all the forensic activity at the airport and Macleod had reluctantly let Curtis reopen, which meant instead of going out to Julia Fluke, he was going to have to talk to her at the airport. He took the paper that Clarissa was handing him, watched as she explained what was going on, but then stood up and announced she'd have to go as Julia Fluke was about to come off the desk.

'Are you sure he opened up again?' asked Clarissa. 'I haven't heard anything.'

'Well, no. I guess people weren't expecting it to open quite so soon, but they are open.'

He walked out of the airport terminal, picking up Hope on the way, and together, they stood at the gate waiting for Julia to come across from the air traffic tower. A tall woman, not quite reaching Hope's six feet, but she certainly had a swagger about her. Dressed in a t-shirt with a baseball jacket on, Macleod could see the blue jeans and the long boots, noting that the air traffic controllers didn't seem to work in any sort of uniform. Instead, most of them seemed to be just left to their own devices.

As Julia opened the gate, Macleod stepped forward, introducing himself. 'I'm Detective Inspector Seoras Macleod. This is Detective Sergeant Hope McGrath. It's good to meet you. If you come with us, we'll just get a room in the airport terminal. Have you had anything to eat? I don't want to keep you from your lunch either. I guess you're going back over to work again soon.'

'Well, no' said Julia, 'because we've come in late in the day so actually, my shift would be over now, normally. Well, my time on the desk anyway. I'm just kicking about for a while, so I'm all yours, Inspector.'

The woman gave a smile and showed a pair of brilliant white teeth. Macleod let the women walk in front of them and Hope engaged Julia on some rather banal chat about how long she'd been at the airport. It had been over five years, and the woman seemed well established, but Macleod noted how light the conversation was which surprised him, given that one of her co-workers had been brutally murdered in the tower.

Once inside, Macleod let Julia pick up a sandwich before

they sat in a quiet office with white walls.

'Sorry to ask you this, Miss Fluke, but how did you get on with John Epson?'

'We got on fine but, to be honest, me and John didn't see eye to eye in terms of our work environment. I disagreed at times with him, but not with anything else. Didn't really know the guy that well. It's funny that you work with people but you just don't understand where they come from sometimes. He was very officious. I'm much more laid back when it comes to the controlling. As for outside of work, I don't think he had any interests that matched mine. At least I never saw him in any activities that I do.'

'What are those?' asked Hope.

'Well, I like to go for walks. Might do a bit of trekking, things like that. I've got to stay fit somehow, haven't I?'

Macleod saw her grin at Hope, but he saw his sergeant was not grinning back. 'On the day in question, you weren't in work, were you?' asked Macleod.

'Oh, the last time we were open when Eppy died? No, I wasn't in work. That was my day off. That's how the cycle fell.'

'What did you do, particularly in the afternoon?' asked Macleod.

'Well, I was out walking, basically. Like I say, keeps you fit. Why? Am I a suspect?'

'It's just routine inquiries,' said Macleod. 'I like to eliminate everybody on a point of evidence as opposed to simply from their word. It keeps everything nice and neat. Did you have anyone that was with you when you were walking?'

'No, I didn't' said Julia, 'but you could try the guy over the road from the house. He's always watching what I'm doing. Saucy devil.' Julia smiled again. Once more, Hope didn't seem to react.

'Do you have any thoughts on why Mr Epson would be the target of a killer?'

'None whatsoever,' she said. 'I know he upset some people with how officious he was and the fact that he liked things done properly. He also didn't treat Curtis very well. Considered him to be an idiot, which may have merit, but the man's still the boss. You can't walk all over him. Well, you can but you shouldn't.'

'Curtis James had got a record of keeping a good eye on the women in the workplace,' said Hope. 'Did you ever have any problems with him?'

'Curtis? Well, yes, he does, doesn't he? But I think I scare him. A bit too big for his taste.'

Macleod assumed the woman could only mean in the physical strength because when it came to having excess weight, she seemed to have none.

'He didn't resent that at all? There wasn't any time when Mr Epson stood in the way of Curtis's advances towards you?'

'Eppy didn't need to stand in the way. If there was trouble with Curtis, Eppy could just brush him off. He's not difficult to handle.'

'Have you ever heard about any drugs coming through the area?' asked Hope.

'Well, you hear about it. Of course, you do. Police have been here with their dogs on occasion, but I haven't seen any and I don't know how they would bring them in.'

'What about Sarah Pullet?' asked Macleod. 'Did you have any issues with her?'

'Well, she thought the rest of us were up our own backsides, I know that. I think she was just someone with a chip on her shoulder against the world. She hadn't been born into anything. Had to work for it and ended up doing a crummy cleaning job. She'd got right upset if you asked her to clean stuff too. Thought you were having a go at her all the time.'

'Do you know of any reason why someone would kill her though?' asked Macleod.

Julia Fluke shook her head, letting her hair swing down around her and again. Macleod saw her glance at Hope.

'Did you think she was beneath you?' asked Hope.

'No,' said Julia. 'We don't think like that these days. Eppy didn't like her though, I know that. Curtis did because she was a woman. The rest of us just never really bothered with her. It was the easiest way, really. She was difficult to make conversation with. She used to come up and just clean. If we said anything, we got a grump. That was it. I guess she really didn't like us.'

'Do you know of any reason why someone would want to kill Sarah Pullet though?' asked Hope.

'I don't know. I mean, to kill somebody, I mean, I thought Curtis might get annoyed with her if she stood up to his advances but the man's quite pathetic. I doubt he would do something like that. Although, I guess you never can tell.'

'That's true,' said Macleod, 'but better if we had some evidence. Have you ever handled a knife?' asked Macleod.

'Well, of course,' said Julia.

'I meant in a more professional sense. Maybe as a soldier or as a chef.'

'No,' said Julia. 'Never. In truth, I'm just glad to get back into work, to get going at things again. John's death has kind of upset everybody, but I guess it won't be long before we'll be back to normal. This is the start of it today.'

Macleod nodded, asked a few more questions, and then let the woman go. As he opened the door for her and let her go out of the room, he saw Hope staring at him. He closed the door behind him, walked over and stood beside the desk, looking down at Hope.

'You were very cool towards her,' said Macleod. 'Is something up?'

'Two things, really.'

'Two?' said Macleod. 'Well, I noticed she was looking at you quite a bit. I know I don't have the experience of that,' he said, 'but I did think she was.'

'Oh, she was looking,' said Hope. 'She's definitely more into women than men. But I wouldn't make a great deal out of her looking at me and not you. Instead, I'd focus on this. I've seen her face before. When I was over at Zoe's, she was in one of the photographs and she had Zoe in a large embrace, and not one of the friendly ones. One of the ones that say, 'Oh yes, she's mine.''

'Well, they haven't said anything to us, but maybe we need to look into these things a bit further. It does bother me about Curtis James though. He seems to be on the periphery of everything.'

'Indeed,' said Hope, 'but is it a case of someone clamouring for attention, or is it someone trying to cover up?'

Chapter 15

C larissa was stumped; she checked the flights coming through and she couldn't see any repetition, anything that showed some sort of a pattern. Part of her wondered if anything was being held back, and so she decided that she was going to have a thorough search of the premises, including the airport manager's office. She knocked on the door and received a slightly taut, 'Come in.'

As she pushed it open and stepped inside, she saw Curtis James glance over at her and caught almost a look of disappointment. *Clearly too old for him*, thought Clarissa. *The man doesn't know quality when he sees it.*

'Mr James, I've been doing some searching through the airport records and I'm not sure I've got everything. I was just going to come in and have a look through your office if that's okay?'

'It's a bit inconvenient, actually,' he said.

'Oh, you won't notice me, don't worry about a thing,' said Clarissa stepping forward.

'Have you got a warrant for this?'

'Do I need one?' asked Clarissa. 'Is there something I'm going to find?'

'You should have a warrant though; I think I might make you ask for a warrant.'

'So, you have got something to hide, Mr James? That's what I thought while we're homing in on you.'

'I'm sorry. You're homing in on me?'

'Well, you want the airport open as quick as possible, you've got your wish on that. Now you want everything to go back to normal. We've got two dead bodies, two people have been brutally murdered and yet you seem to be giving me the brush off, so I'm going to come in here and have a look, whether I come in with a warrant later, or you let me search now. I believe you keep some of the records here in a safe.'

'Who told you that?' asked Curtis.

'A bit of rumour floating about said that Curtis keeps something locked up in his safe. I'm sure there's certain things you can't share with the staff around here; it's only right that the manager has his own privacy. Unfortunately, that privacy doesn't extend to murder investigations. Maybe it's your personal thoughts on people, something like that. It's just at the moment we've got a drugs angle, and we're just wondering what sort of information is kept regards to the planes coming through. I've looked at what's officially there and I'm not able to work anything out from it, so I wondered if there was anything unofficial. Any visits? Any sort of diaries?'

Clarissa saw Curtis choke, and he raised himself up. 'I do have a diary but it's personal; it's kept in the safe.'

'And there's nothing in this diary that's incriminating, I take it?' said Clarissa. The man almost jumped. 'That's not a resounding no,' said Clarissa. 'With the way you're reacting, I feel I need to have a look at this diary. Of course, if it's got nothing to do with the case, it'll remain discreet, between you and me. However, I'm not sure that's what we're going to find.'

'You can't look at it,' said Curtis. 'This is my private safe; it's my things to keep.'

'What's in the diary then?' asked Clarissa.

'I can't say, I'm not telling.' The man almost turned away, coiling up like a little child.

'Right then,' said Clarissa, 'on that basis I am going to go and get a warrant to search these offices because clearly, you don't want me to. I believe you're withholding information that may be pertinent to the case. A warrant is coming. However, I'm going to station somebody here so that you can't sneak away with anything from that safe.'

'You can't do that.'

'Can't do what? Put somebody in front of your office to make sure you don't walk away with stuff? Not a problem. I can do that. You practically said to me that this is incriminating evidence that's contained in the diary. There's no way I'm letting that go.'

'But then people will see; there'll be loads of people knowing something's going on in the office.'

'Yes,' said Clarissa, 'absolutely, that'll be because there is something going on in the office. Would you like me to do that or are you going to let me have a look now?'

Clarissa could see the man raging inside, and he stood up from behind his desk, turned around and thumped it so hard that Clarissa thought he'd hurt himself. 'It's wrong,' he said, 'these are private things.'

'This is a murder investigation,' said Clarissa. 'We lift everything up and shake it out. Kindly open the safe for me or I'm straight out of here for a warrant and trust me, everybody will see that I've got men posted around this room to stop you running off with things.' The man started to go red, and Clarissa knew she had him. When he turned and undid the safe, she smiled to herself.

'If you just kindly step aside, Mr James, I'll have a look in there.'

Inside the safe were a number of files which showed future projects for the airfield, nothing that Clarissa thought was particularly worth looking into. As far as she could see, the most controversial thing was where the new toilet block was going to go. But there was also a diary and that she took out. She walked over to the window before opening it up and beginning to read. She was aware that Curtis James's eyes were on her, watching her closely as she scanned through.

As she began to read, she noted that most of the women on the airfield seemed to be contained within the diary. The difference was that this was not about anything that had happened. At least if they had, Clarissa would be stunned.

Julia Fluke was mentioned, going for the romantic meal and some activities at her house afterwards. Sarah Pullet, there for a job interview but suddenly descending into something Clarissa would expect to find sitting on the top shelf, amongst a bunch of magazines. Zoe Jillings was also there running around on the beach with not very much on. Kylie Youngs seemed to be in a number of tricky situations all with Curtis.

Clarissa looked over at the man, who was a mixture of rage and a sheepish face, turning away from her every time she looked.

'Interesting reading,' said Clarissa.

'You can see it's got nothing to do with the case,' said Curtis. 'Put it back in and I'll lock the safe up again.'

'No, you won't,' said Clarissa. 'I think we need to go and

have a chat.'

'Why? They're just recreational ideas.'

'One of the women mentioned in your diary is now dead. It makes me wonder if you ever tried to enact any of these fantasies. Some of the women I think would give you a right good punch to the head if they ever knew this existed, but some of the rest might not be so able to defend themselves. You may be able to blackmail them. Mr Epson was a righteous and upstanding man; maybe he knew about this, maybe he'd heard about something. I think you're going to have to wait here, and I'll get the boss to come in.'

Clarissa left the office, and waved over the local constable, telling him to stand at the door and not to let Mr James leave. Clarissa knocked on the door of a separate office to find Macleod and Hope having a discussion, having completed their interview with Julia Fluke.

'Boss, I think you need to come and talk again to Mr James. I found a diary within a safe of his. It basically has a lot of fantasy writing in it.'

'Fantasy writing?' said Hope, 'What? Like dwarves and elves and that?'

'No,' said Clarissa, 'like about women and his sexual prowess with them. All the women in the airport here seem to be mentioned, including Sarah Pullet. I thought with how Mr Epson was seen as being an upstanding man, maybe he'd found out about some of this. Maybe Curtis's coercing them. I thought it best if you and the sergeant have a word.'

'Good work,' said Macleod, 'I'm coming directly. Looks like you've got him this time.'

As Macleod left the room, Hope went over to Clarissa. 'All the women?' she said. 'You didn't check at the back of it. Did

131

you?'

'Why?' asked Clarissa.

'Just in case he's added extra chapters with us.'

Clarissa burst out laughing, causing Macleod to turn around. 'Nothing,' said Clarissa, 'just a woman's joke.'

Macleod shook his head and made his way over to the office of the airport manager. The door was opened for him by the local constable, who he thanked and dismissed. Once inside, he saw Curtis James sitting with his head in his hands at the desk. Clarissa joined Macleod, handing him the diary and it took Macleod only a few minutes of skimming through to confirm what Clarissa had said. He passed it to Hope who he was sure was trying not to smirk as she read it.

'This puts a different complexion on things, Mr James. I asked you before with regard to Kylie Youngs, did you have sex with her in order for her to obtain a position at this airfield? You said no. Would you like to clarify that?'

'I didn't. I didn't, 'he said; 'it's ridiculous. It's just things I write for my own amusement.'

Hope seemed engrossed in the diary at this point, and she marched forward with it placing it down in front of Mr James. 'Do you want to read to the Inspector these couple of pages?' Curtis James shook his head. 'Would that be because they're describing in fairly intimate, if exaggerated, detail, the interview process for Kylie Youngs?'

'Okay,' said Curtis, 'you got me, but she offered. She said, "Is there any way I can . . ." Well, she was . . . well, look at her. You've seen her, haven't you? I mean, who wouldn't?'

'I wouldn't,' said Macleod, 'it's not what people do. You're in a position of influence and power here. You're meant to be a respectable part of the community. The girl's nineteen. She's only been an adult a year or so and while having spoken to her, I believe she was very fully aware of what she was doing, but it's still wrong. An employment tribunal wouldn't be happy with it.

'However, what bothers me more is what happens if they don't come round to this idea. Do you get an idea and then decide you have to do more, that the rest of the women within this place should be following along Kylie Youngs' route? I think she's exceptional. Most women wouldn't go for this.'

'And certainly not with you.'

Macleod looked over at Clarissa. She'd clearly voiced out to what was in her head without meaning to.

'She can't say that,' said Curtis James.

'No, she can't but, as ever, my sergeant, while not being particularly discreet, is probably fundamentally accurate. This gives me cause for concern,' said Macleod, making sure his tone was being imparted, not just to Curtis James but also to his sergeants. 'Some people might look at this and think it as just some sort of romp, but I don't. It gives me great concern about what happened to Sarah Pullet. What happened to Mr Epson? Did he find out about any of this? Was he liable to blow the whistle? This information gives me cause to put you up as a suspect, someone with a motive. I can't prove it at the moment, but it does give me cause for further investigation.'

Macleod spun on his heel to the sergeants behind him. 'McGrath, Urquhart, I want you to go into Mr James's house and I want you to search it from top to bottom.'

'You can't do that,' said Curtis James.

'Why?' asked Macleod. 'I've just told you why—you've been elevated up our suspect list. I need to check that out and I need to make sure that you are just a dirty old man and not someone who's been compromised in a much bigger fashion.'

'But she's in, Ellie's in.'

'Ellie?' asked Macleod.

'Ellie James,' said Hope. 'It'll be his wife.'

'Well, well, you better hope we don't find anything,' said Macleod. 'You don't want to own up yet to any more diaries at home?'

'Why would I keep a diary at home? Why do you think it's in the damn safe?'

'I take it it's not a broad relationship you have then, with your wife?' said Hope.

'Well, I'm coming with you,' said Curtis James. 'I'm not having you speaking to her without me.'

'Why?' asked Macleod, suddenly and sharply. 'Why not?'

'Because she . . . she . . .'

'She what?'

'She doesn't know about this. I'm not having you drop things in, then I'll get home, and I won't be able to explain it to her.'

'You think you'll be able to explain this now?' said Clarissa.

Macleod turned on his heel again to the sergeants. 'Urquhart, McGrath, get down that house now. I'm going to stay here and have a word with Mr James. Give me a ring with what you've found. We'll be waiting here.'

Macleod made sure his sergeants left the room, ensuring that Clarissa didn't make some witty comment. He could understand it. The guy was a lecherous clown, and Macleod would never have been the focus of any of his attentions. Hope possibly. Even Clarissa might have been so. Therefore, to kick the man when he was down, seemed to be a very reasonable, if unprofessional, response.

Macleod turned back to Curtis James. He was now sitting

134

back in his seat, his hands over his head.

'When they come back and tell me what they've found, I want you to have told me before them. If not, my opinion of you is going to be far worse, so I'm here. Curtis, speak to me.'

Chapter 16

Clarissa's green sports car pulled up alongside a rather large house, which was out on its own in the country, with two splendid pillars at the front. Clearly, it hadn't been built a long time ago but looked rather more modern. As Clarissa stepped out of the car, closing the door behind her, she looked up to see the front door opening. Hope joined Clarissa and the two women walked their way up the driveway, one head and shoulders above the other. It was Clarissa who was at the front marching on straight up to the woman who was coming out. She had blonde hair, which was neatly permed and tucked around a rather lined forehead. The woman wasn't petite, and her large shoulders were raised up.

'What do you want? Curtis said you wouldn't come here.'

'We're here to search the premises. Now kindly step aside,' said Clarissa.

'Search the premises? You'll do no such thing.'

'Why?' asked Clarissa; 'you have something to hide? We're simply going to be looking to see if there's anything strange in the house. If you turn us away, we'll get a warrant. Although your husband's already given us permission to do this. When we come back, it won't be us. It'll be a lot more people, very public.'

Although Clarissa was aware there was nobody about, the road they were on did lead directly to Tobermory so traffic would be passing by.

'If you must,' said the woman, very contentiously, 'but I'm not happy about this and be careful with everything. The stuff in here costs money. Not like something you would get in your house.'

Clarissa raised her eyebrows at the woman and then strode straight past her towards the open door.

'But why are you here?' asked the woman as they entered the house.

'Would you mind telling me where your husband spends most of his time in the house?' asked Clarissa.

'Why? What is up?'

'We're here to search the house,' said Clarissa. 'I've already told you that. Where does your husband spend most of his time?'

'Up in the back,' she said. 'That's his game room, so to speak.'

'Thank you,' said Clarissa, and marched off up the stairs but found the woman continued to follow her.

'Is he playing around on me?'

'I'm sorry?' asked Clarissa.

'I said, "Is he playing around on me?"'

'That's not what we're here to investigate,' said Hope. 'We're here for investigations into the murder of John Epson and Sarah Pullet.'

'He didn't take to Sarah dying very well.'

'How do you mean?' asked Clarissa.

'Well, I'm sure he was looking at her. He looked at them all. He does, doesn't he? When he's out and about with me, he's always looking, always checking out someone else.'

'That may be so but we're here to check the rooms he's been in and to conduct a search,' said Hope. 'Are you correct? This top one is the one you say we should go to? This is where he spends his time?'

'Yes, but you'll laugh when you go in.'

Clarissa opened the door, took one look inside, and then held her arms open for Hope to join her.

As Hope walked past, Clarissa whispered, 'The woman does not lie.' Hope entered into a room that was long and reasonably thin. Inside were large amounts of circus equipment from magician boxes to a small trapeze hanging from the ceiling.

'What on earth's all this?' asked Hope.

'This is him. This is what he's into,' spat his wife. Hope looked around and saw pictures on the wall. The same man was in every single one of them. Yet, in most, he had a woman on his arm, at times, holding them in a fashion that may no longer be considered appropriate. From assistants dressed in bikinis to people who had obviously been in the audience, there were a plethora of photographs of the man.

'Who is that?' asked Hope.

Ellie James gave a shake of her head. 'Curtis's Uncle. Curtis idolised him. He used to come up and collect Curtis for the summer, take him back to his place as a kid. It was all about the circus, all about the magic acts or the knife throwing. Knife throwing was the big one.'

Clarissa's ears perked up. She glanced over at Hope.

'Yes, knife throwing but he got the trapeze and everything else. His uncle was a womaniser. I mean, look at the photographs. It's like something from the seventies, the way he's treating some of those women. There they are, fawning all over him. Curtis used to be like that with me. We used to have our photograph taken and I'd be the woman in his arms, but it didn't bother me because we were on our own. Then I started seeing him trying to do the same with other women. His eyes are everywhere. I think he takes after his uncle. Is he cheating on me?'

'There's nothing wrong with this,' said Clarissa. 'I grant you that those photographs look rather creepy, but this is just a hobby. It's a form of theatre, the circus. That's what you've got here. There's not anything here to say that he's cheating on you. Although I'll give you, your husband does have a rather rampant mind.'

'Are you married?' Ellie asked Clarissa.

'No, but I've been around about men long enough.'

'What about you?' she asked Hope.

'Not married, I do have a partner.'

'What's he do?'

'He works in the car-hire business.'

'Does he have hobbies like this?'

'Not that I'm aware of,' said Hope.

'Well, maybe you'll be a lucky one then.'

Clarissa was making her way through the circus items. As she bent down into a large trunk that was on the floor, flicking open the clasps, Clarissa looked down inside. There was a purple piece of material running the entire length of the box and she moved it back slowly before realising that she was looking at the handle of a blade. Pulling back the material slightly more, she saw that the blade of the knife below was a diamond in shape.

'Sergeant McGrath, come over here.'

Hope appeared at Clarissa's shoulder and looked down.

'Let's get it covered up.'

'What's the matter?' asked the woman. 'What's wrong?'

'I'll have to ask you to step out of the room,' said Hope. 'We've got to seal this room off and we're going to have forensic come and take a look.'

'Why? What's he done?'

'We don't know yet but like I say we are investigating the murder of two people.'

'Did your husband ever talk about work?' asked Clarissa.

'Talk about work?' said Ellie. 'It's all he ever talks about. Himself and well—'

'What?'

'He doesn't think he does it, but he does. There's a young lass, works as an assistant, Kylie; he mentions her all the time, as well as most of the other women.'

'What about Harold Lyme and John Epson?'

'Barely mentions them at all. You see my husband is very, very like his uncle—he's a prig. His uncle was an arrogant prig and Curtis idolised the man. He talked to women like Curtis talks to them now. They're an addiction to him and I'm sick of it, and I'm sick of this nonsense.'

Hope gently steered the woman out of the room as Clarissa closed the door behind them and got on her phone.

'We've just got to call our boss who will send forensics down here very, very soon. We'll do our best not to disturb you.'

'When's he coming home?' asked Ellie.

'To be honest with you, a lot depends on what we find and what forensics say. I take it he's had this setup for a while.'

'This is the scaled-down version. There was much more stuff than this, but I told him to get rid of it. He took it away to the dump one day and he was in a foul mood with me because of it. I don't know if you noticed, there's a large number of assistant costumes up there. He wanted me to wear those as well—no chance.'

'What's the fascination with his uncle then?'

'Well, he does like the circus stuff,' said Ellie, 'but his uncle also had a lot of groupies around him, and I think that's what Curtis likes. He used to be different the first five, maybe ten years I knew him but then, as he was getting older, he realised that other people, other women no longer looked at him. Maybe I got older, a touch fatter, or something else, but he just didn't want me anymore. He would tell you, he thought he was subtle about it but the one thing he isn't is subtle. I think Curtis always thought he should be like his uncle and then they would just arrive but he hasn't done well with the job. A lot of them see him as a comedy figure up there. I just hope he hasn't, that he hasn't . . .'

'He hasn't what?' asked Clarissa.

'Gone and done something stupid. Dear God, he hasn't done something stupid, has he?'

The woman leaned forward, burying her face into the shawl wrapped around Clarissa's shoulder. Clarissa could feel the tears beginning, and she held the woman tight allowing her to cry for a moment while Hope ran off to finish her phone call. When the woman had settled down, Clarissa handed her a handkerchief to wipe her eyes and sat her down in the sofa downstairs. As she sat beside her, Clarissa ran her eyes across the woman's face. The woman had come out initially all fire and brimstone but now Clarissa saw someone who clearly still had a love for her husband, even if she realised how much of a lecherous man he was.

'I'm sorry,' she said, 'but two people are dead.'

141

'I know,' said Clarissa. 'I'm used to this, but you're not and it is a shock. I need to ask you something though. Those knives up there, where do they come from?'

'Most of this was Curtis's uncle's, but the knives especially. Curtis was taught how to throw them. People put up on a wheel and spun round and he would fire the knives at them and miss every time. I've been up on it, I used to do it when I was younger with Curtis. Oh, he used to love it. He'd come up and he'd make this whole to-do thing about people watching and he was up on the stage with me. Of course, there was no one there; it just rolled into his fantasies after that. To be honest, he even seemed to enjoy the knife-throwing bit more than any of the other, even more than what happened afterwards? You'd have thought that that was the bit he wanted to get to. The bit where we got, how do you put it?'

'Intimate?' said Clarissa.

Inside she felt proud for a moment. She was going to say, 'Squishy,' but intimate was definitely the correct word. Macleod would have been proud of her for that too.

'Yes, intimate. He's a strange man, my husband, very strange. In a lot of ways, he means well, but he just, he just . . . damn him,' she said. Then she picked up an ornament beside her and flung it off the wall, causing it to smash. Hope raced into the room, looked over at Clarissa, who put her hand up waving, indicating that nothing was amiss. Hope left the room.

Ellie turned around to Clarissa again. 'Sorry,' she said. 'It's just that he's . . . it's just that . . .' Her hand reached out, grabbing another one and went to throw it but Clarissa reached up, grabbed the woman's wrist before it could go anywhere, and with her other hand, she took what the woman was about to throw off the wall.

'I wouldn't do that. I think this is Georgian, it's probably worth a small fortune. I don't like to see antiques destroyed.'

'But you let me throw the first one.'

'Indeed, I did; you picked that one up off a market stall. Just settle down, love, and promise me, you're not going to smash anything else.' The woman nodded and Clarissa heard the arrival of the forensic van outside. The day wasn't getting better for Ellie James.

Chapter 17

Hope jumped out of the squad car and walked over to the terminal building, marching directly to the airport manager's office where Macleod was still sitting with Curtis James. As she opened the door, she could see Curtis looking over, anxious. Macleod stood up and came over to take Hope to one side.

'Well, what did you find?' he asked quietly.

'You're not going to believe this. He's got a whole room of like circus stuff, including knife throwing.'

'Knife throwing? Why? Look at him. You'd never think he was a knife thrower.'

'Apparently, his uncle used to take him away in summer holidays and his uncle was all into this. Bit of a star, by the looks of it. He had women falling off his arm. I reckon that's where the man's got taught his manners, or lack of them anyway. There were loads of photographs up of his uncle during the time when he used to perform, after show, pre-show, women on his arm here, there, and everywhere. I think our Curtis's a little bit off in the head. Seems to think that's the way it works, that's what will happen with women. Might have been back in the day and even then, probably only a certain type. It certainly wouldn't happen now.'

'Must have been a dream to him when Kylie Youngs pitched up and made an offer.'

'I'm sure it was, Seoras, but the thing is, did he actually kill anyone? We've got Jona looking at the knives. I don't know if they're the same or not. They look like throwing knives, but let's leave it to the expert.'

'The trouble is, Hope, look at him.'

Hope looked over Macleod's shoulder. 'Yes, I know what you mean, Seoras. I can see him as a lech. I can see him as a man who might throw his weight around, a bit of a bully, but if anyone stood up to him, he'd crumble. Look at him. I mean, what woman is going to take him? I also don't think he's got the killer instinct, not to go through with it. The planning, everything about it. When we spoke to the air traffic people, they all said he was a clown. He couldn't handle the responsibility of the aerodrome. It just doesn't sit right, does it?'

'No, it doesn't,' said Macleod, 'but my problem is this. At the moment, the evidence is pointing to him. It's circumstantial. We can't prove he was there, but it's definitely pointing at him.'

'Is it meant to?' asked Hope. She stepped past Macleod. 'I'd be careful when you go home tonight,' said Hope. 'That's if you are going home, of course.'

'What do you mean by that?' asked Curtis.

'Our issue is,' said Macleod, approaching from behind Hope, 'everything's pointing to you. We've got the knives up at your house. Apparently, you've got throwing knives. We didn't tell anyone that the knives we found were throwing knives, but they were sharp, used to cut through the neck. Lo and behold, we found throwing knives at your house. We found out you were trained to use them.'

'I was trained to throw them at somebody spinning round, not stand behind someone and cut their throat out.'

'Doesn't matter. You still know how to use them, how to sharpen them.'

'You don't sharpen them. That's the point. Anyway, why would I have turned up at Sarah Pullet's?'

'Double bluff,' said Hope. 'It happens. You have to be aware of it as a police officer.' Curtis looked dejected, put his hands on the desk, planted his face into his arms, and started to cry.

'What I don't know is why you would kill Mr Epson. Everyone said you had angry debates about the aerodrome but why? It doesn't make sense. Nobody said he belittled you in front of anyone. Unless you took offense. Unless you're not living up to standards you thought you should have, or was it one of the women that did it? Maybe Epson backed them up.'

'No,' said Curtis. He started slamming his hands on the desk. 'No, no, no. I didn't do any of this. I didn't kill anyone. Yes, I wrote a whole lot of fabricated stories about just about every woman in this place. Yes, I slept with Kylie Youngs, but only because she offered it. I didn't grab her.'

Macleod pulled Hope away, moving to the corner of the room.

'Are you going to arrest him?'

'No,' said Macleod. 'We'll keep him in for questioning. This could grow arms and legs very quickly and we need to make sure. Jona hasn't come up with anything yet. I'm hoping that she might soon. We've got Ross looking into aircraft details as well. I know Clarissa looked at it, but Ross is a bit more thorough. He sees the patterns we don't.'

'Well, I'll let you tell her that,' said Hope. Macleod rolled his eyes at her. He felt the phone vibrating in his pocket and picked it up.

'Macleod here.'

'Inspector, Jona. Just to let you know, I've examined the throwing knives. They're not the same. The knives I have here are blunt, but more than that, they're not the same type of knife. They look similar, but they're not the same.'

'So, what? They're not from that set?'

'Definitely not, but the other two are the same set. The two that were used to kill are the same set.'

'You're telling me that Curtis isn't the killer?'

'That's your department. What I'm telling you is that the knives found in his room in his house are not the same as the knives that were used to kill. Beyond that, I have no evidence. Hopefully, I'm going to be able to get you some idea of what the killer was like. We found some bruising on the bodies. I just need a little time to look into it. Might be able to get you an idea of maybe the hand size of the killer, or even a notion of whether it was a man or a woman.'

'Okay,' said Macleod. 'Keep on it. Let me know when you've got something.' There was a rap at the door which opened and then Ross stuck his head in.

'Sir, sorry to disturb you, but I could really do with talking to you right now.'

'Where?' asked Macleod.

'Come back to my office. I've got some data I'd like you to look at. Might help move things on.'

'Okay. Hope, sit with Mr James and see if he can come up with anything else that'll help us clear his name.'

Hope rolled her eyes at Macleod. Clearly, she would prefer if one of the uniforms came in and sat with him. He didn't

147

blame her, with the man's record. Macleod could see Curtis staring at her. On the other hand, he wanted someone in the room who could tell him if Curtis had let something slip, and Hope was the person for that.

Macleod followed Ross across the airport terminal to another office where Ross slid in front of his laptop.

'I've been looking at records, sir. The thing is, we're getting no planes that come through that are passing on a regular basis. Everything's pretty ad hoc, except for the commercial flights, the schedules. The scheduled traffic comes in and out every day; that's pretty normal. If you're carrying drugs on them, you're highly likely to get caught because you're going through airport security. Therefore, to bring drugs in, if you're going to fly it in, you're going to come to the smaller apron where you don't have to go through security to get there.'

'Okay, still with you,' said Macleod. 'So what?'

'When I looked at the planes that have come into the small apron, I found there's no repeat traffic at all.'

'So, you're saying the drugs aren't coming in through the airport?' said Macleod.

'That's not what I'm saying,' said Ross. 'You have to look deeper. This was where Sergeant Urquhart was having problems. If you trace back the aircraft, understand not just who owns them but actually who is flying them, you soon get to where you want to go.'

'You're losing me, Ross. What do you mean?'

'Okay, I'll put it simply,' said Ross. 'There's a company that flies through here all the time. They deal in ferry flights. The aircraft each time is different, but it's the same company flying the aircraft even though the aircraft owner is different. That company, for some reason, is bringing their flights into

Stornoway and then down to here, before heading on to Blackpool. The company itself is based in Blackpool. What I don't understand is why they want to fly into here. They can easily make Blackpool with the types of aircraft that are coming in, as most of them are light twins. Even the single-engine ones are reasonably sized aircraft and could complete the run from Stornoway down quite easily, and there are probably better airports to fly into if they did want to put in a stop.'

'How long do they stay on the ground for?' asked Macleod.

'We're looking at the flight plans and the departures. They're lucky if they're on the ground for an hour.'

'So, you're thinking they come in, possibly drop the drugs off?'

'That was my thinking, but if they did it, it would be airside. Now, they might be able to go up to the terminal building, drop them off there, but you're either going to do it in the car park, or you're going to do it in the terminal building, or you're going to do it with somebody who is allowed to be on the airside of the airfield.'

'So, someone that was in the air traffic tower?'

'Or the fire station,' said Ross. 'or one of the local pilots, although there's not many of them.'

'Do any of these people arrive and come over to the tower?'

'I'm not sure.' Macleod looked over at a phone sitting beside Ross' desk and asked if he could use it. Ross nodded. Macleod picked it up and pressed the zero for the switchboard. From there, he asked for the air traffic tower and got Harold Lyme on the other end.

'Hello, Inspector. How can I help you?'

'I'm just wondering; you get these ferry flights that come

through. Does anybody ever come over to the air traffic tower?'

'You get the occasional visitor. Sometimes you get people who want to go round all the towers. It's like a tourist thing.'

'I was thinking more for general sorts of needs.'

'General needs?' said Harold. 'I'm not quite with you. Do you mean like what if they need the loo?'

'Yes, that's it.'

'Well, they can use the terminal building because it's got toilets up there, but yes, if they want to have a quick in and out, they will come over and use our toilets on occasion. It saves them having to go onto the landside and then get the security to bring them back down to the apron.'

'So, the security wouldn't see them at all?' said Macleod.

'No, not at all. There's no need.'

'Where do they pay their landing fees, these people? I understand that you'd pay money to land an aircraft at an airfield.'

'That's right. Some of them are on account and get it billed to them, so they won't necessarily have to come over here. The small ones, they're only paying fifteen or twenty quid. They'll come over and drop it, but the ferry flights, it depends, but most of them will be paying on account. We've got their address.'

'Do you see any of that up in the tower?'

'No. That's routed through the accounts people. We just note the aircraft registration, et cetera. They usually book in if they're coming through anyway. All the details are there. Money disappears, I assume, through bank accounts. They get billed in a normal way to any aircraft company.'

'Okay,' said Macleod. 'That's interesting. Thank you.'

'What was that all about, sir?' asked Ross.

'Just following up on your theory. You could come in here in a ferry flight because you've come from another airport within the UK, and if you've come off their smaller aprons or the ones that don't require security, you can land here. You don't have to go landside; you could come in and be using the toilets. There's nothing to say that you couldn't come in and drop a couple of kilos of drugs in the top of the cistern or somewhere else. Then somebody in here can go and pick it up.

'Once they picked it up, they'd be going out to the car and driving off. It would look perfectly normal. If they took the drugs out to the car park or up to the terminal, there's always the risk they're going to get seen, but not if they bring it inside the building. Why are people going to bat an eye at a pilot coming into a building with a flight bag? We're not saying that he has to do that; he can put it in his jacket. He's a pilot coming over. Nothing unusual there.'

'What about the police dogs and stuff? They use sniffers, do they not?'

'They are more concerned with the commercial, the scheduled traffic, I think. These people are coming through very rarely. At the end of the day, if you've got somebody here and they see the police dogs about, all you do is turn around and make up a reason for going to a different airfield.'

'It's an interesting idea, sir, but you've got no proof of it.'

'No, I don't,' said Macleod, 'but we know that this flight came from Stornoway and then went down to Blackpool, the company's base. Who is the company, by the way?'

'Jefferson Aviation,' said Ross.

'Well, Jefferson Aviation, they'll know all the pilots that come through here. We can see if it's the same person. We can tie down maybe one or two that are passing through. We can also find out why they come here.'

'Well, that's a question to be asked, isn't it? I guess you're wanting me to get on the phone?'

'No,' said Macleod. We've still got a flight that's going to get out of here tonight, haven't we?' Ross nodded. 'Good. I think I need to send down someone who can shake them up a bit. Get to the core of it. You're good, Ross, on the old computer. I mean when it comes to following a trail like this, there's no one I'd rather have, but if we're going down there to try and confront somebody about running drugs, I think we need someone with a bit more clout.' Ross sat back and looked up at Macleod, almost annoyed.

'Well, don't take it like that. I'm not sending Hope. I'm sending Clarissa. The good thing is she doesn't fully understand how this aviation thing works, so she'll badger them. She'll go in like a blunt instrument, knocking aside all arguments, making them say it in black and white, and she'll get to the bottom of it. You wait and see, Ross. It's time to let her loose.'

Chapter 18

Hope was not particularly enamoured at having to babysit Curtis James, and when she sat down opposite him at the desk, she saw him raise his head, staring at her, and part of her felt distinctly uncomfortable. If she had been in a bar, she'd have said some words to the man, or even gone over and given him a clip, but she was a serving officer and that kind of thing was frowned upon. So instead, she picked up the diary and began to read it in front of him.

She watched him begin to squirm, and so she kept reading it, keeping the room in silence. As Hope flicked through it, she found one particular section interesting, concerning Julia Fluke. She was seen as one of the stronger women, and from what Macleod had said, she cut rather an impressive figure, not simply in how she looked.

As she started to read about Curtis James's fantasy about Julia, she was quite interested to find out that the poor woman was heading towards the circus big top. In the story, she was taken from the audience at the circus, before being taken backstage and dressed in what Hope thought was a rather sexualised outfit for what was pretending to be a family show. One thing that struck Hope, though, was the man's writing style was actually quite good. Although what he was describing was, by all standards, leery, the manner in which he did it was almost eloquent. She reckoned he must have had a silver tongue.

In his younger day, was he was the one who tried to come up to the women, chat them up? Did he have more success back then? Maybe it was something she could ask his wife. Although quite how responsive she'd be at the moment, given the current circumstances, Hope didn't know.

In the story, Julia returned to the big top, was put on a spinning wheel, and had knives thrown at her, all missing except the occasional one that seemed to cause a wardrobe malfunction. Hope shook her head as she read it. Then her eyes flicked up, and she saw Curtis staring at her. She almost snarled at him, and he bent over, hiding his face away from her.

Macleod was right, she thought, *when he's confronted, he's backing down, he's backing away. He's like a bully trying to be impressive, but suddenly fading like a flower when somebody has the audacity to bite back. They said that in the tower as well. He came up with his great ideas, and they'd just shoot him down.* Hope wondered if that was why some of the women were treated in his tales in the way they were.

Macleod walked back into the room, and Hope stood up, almost running over to him.

'I've had a thought,' she said. 'I'd like to go and see Kylie again, see if I can go at her, get a little bit more out of her. Woman to woman, so to speak.'

'Why?' asked Macleod.

'In here, Curtis's got a tale about Julia. Now Julia takes part in a circus act that quite frankly goes off the scale, but I reckon our man here might have looked to play out that particular act for real, or some sort of thing like it? The knives aren't the same back at home, but why would you keep knives at home that were the same?' asked Hope. 'Maybe he hasn't got a place at home where he could bring a lady. After all, he is married, Seoras.'

'So, you think he might have somewhere else? Somewhere where he can live out some of these fantasies with anyone who's what, willing?'

'Look at him. I mean, this is what he is. I know part of us don't want to go in and explore this, but we're going to have to,' said Hope. 'We want to find out if he did it; you and I are both sitting thinking he's a clown without the stomach for this, but do you know what? We need to prove that.

'If he's being set up, somebody knows about this fetish or whatever it is he's got. Somebody knows about the knives. We need to trace that. How do they know? Why do they know? His stuff is up in the back of the house. I haven't seen anything around the airport that would give that hobby away, and he certainly wouldn't have been showing this diary to anyone either.'

'Okay,' said Macleod. 'Just to let you know, I'm sending Clarissa to Blackpool.'

'Really? Why does she get a holiday?' asked Hope.

'One of the ferry flights that come through here, Ross did a good job and traced one that has repeat ferry flights, different aircraft but same company. We can't understand why they're landing here. I have a hunch it might be to do with the drugs.'

'And you thought you'd send down the hound to sort it out?' Hope suddenly reddened.

Macleod glared at Hope. 'I would never call Detective

Sergeant Urquhart, the hound. You'd better get going before you start making up names for everyone else.'

As Hope walked past him, Macleod whispered, 'It's a pretty accurate one though.' Hope didn't look back but gave a slight smile as she exited the building. Hope took her own car from the car park and drove down to Kylie Youngs' flat. She could see the light was on when she arrived. Pressing the door buzzer, she was allowed to enter and climbed the stairs up to the flat. When the flat door was opened, Kylie stood looking at her, wrapped up in a tight T-shirt and some leggings.

'Kind of hoping your boss was here,' she said to Hope.

'Why?'

'Kind of cute, isn't he? All serious and all that, real gentleman. He came in to interview me, and I was working away on the bike. Then I was going for a shower, and he's stepping out of the way, a bit of old school.'

'Inspector Macleod's very old school. He's got great respect for women,' said Hope. 'He wouldn't have thought you walking around like that was particularly modern; he'd have seen it as very provocative.'

'Good,' said Kylie, 'I like it when I can get under their skin.'

Hope cocked her head to one side, and then give her a wry smile. The girl certainly was what she was, a complete flirt. In fact, more than a flirt. *But you know what?* thought Hope. *At least she is what she is; honest about it.*

'Do you mind if I come in for a chat?' said Hope. 'I just want to ask you a few questions about Curtis James.'

'Oh, him. He was too easy. I did that for the job. I like men, I make no bones about it, but somebody like Curtis, that was for the job.'

'I understand that,' said Hope, 'and I'm in no way criticizing you for it, but I was just wondering did Curtis want anything else?'

'Curtis wasn't getting anything else,' said Kylie, 'full stop! That man got sex to get me a job, and he got it once. He was told that was the deal. He wasn't coming back for more. He wasn't going to blackmail me because if he did, I was going straight to his missus and explaining exactly what he had just accepted.

'A quiet fighter under there, isn't there,' said Hope. 'I find it quite funny. The way you just handle him.'

'Well, the man's not difficult to handle. Stand up to him, he crumbles, but you were asking about other things. What did you mean?'

'Well, we've learnt that he's a wee bit of a fetishist, likes to have little stories and ideas about women. Especially a lot of you up in the tower. I was just wondering if he'd asked you to do anything more.'

The girl laughed out loud. 'Do you want a coffee?' she said.

'Okay,' said Hope and followed her through where Kylie Youngs made a coffee. They sat down together on the sofa.

'Look,' said Kylie, 'maybe I shouldn't be saying this but when I offered him, you know, to have sex to get the job, he said to me, would I be for dressing up? I'm thinking, *Whoa, now, hang on a minute. What's all this about?* He said to me, "Oh, it's nothing funny. Look." He started showing me pictures of this guy who did a knife-throwing act. He actually wanted me to dress up, in frankly, what didn't look like a very safe outfit. He was going to throw knives and pretend we were in front of an audience.'

'And then what?' asked Hope.

'Then, however it happened, we were going to end up getting

157

it on in front of the whole audience. Of course, there wouldn't be an audience, but he'd be imagining it.'

'What did you say to that?'

Kylie Youngs laughed, got up, and walked over to the window. Hope followed her. 'Do you see this?' said Kylie. 'I had to have—what you would call relations with that man. Trust me. It didn't last more than ten minutes. I'm not proud of it but look at this, look at this view. Look at this flat. I got what I wanted for ten minutes of . . . well, pain's not the word, but you know what I mean? Now, he didn't get what he wanted. He thought he did, but he's probably been sitting dreaming about the whole thing over and over again and hasn't been satisfied at all. That's the thing about him—he's clueless. He doesn't have a clue what he wants or how he wants it.'

'Did it ever get beyond him sort of sketching out an idea?'

'Oh yes. I think it's an idea he's had for a while. I'm not sure he has ever got anywhere with the idea. He wanted me to meet him in an industrial estate, just outside here, on the outskirts of Tobermory. Apparently, he had something there. I don't know if it was in a container or what, or where it is. Whatever he had, it was locked up because he said he'd have to come at night when everything was quiet so clearly, not a lot of people knew about it but there was no way I was doing that.

'We went to a hotel for what I did with him. Booked into a hotel. I made sure somebody knew I was in that room because I'm not daft. He asked me to go to an industrial estate late at night. I count myself lucky, I mean, if it's him, that's done this last lot of stuff. Although I can't see it, he's too weak a man, but with what's gone on, you have to be careful. A girl has got to look after herself.'

'You're right,' said Hope. 'You are right, you do have to look after yourself. For what it's worth, I think you paid too high a price for this flat, but that's your business. You sound smart enough to have made it on your own without it.'

'You only say that because you don't live here. My name's not great around here. Growing up, they didn't think much of me. Got to take what opportunities I can.'

'As long as you don't lose yourself on the way,' said Hope, 'but this industrial estate, did he give you the location of it? Whereabouts was the place he wanted you to go to?'

'He never said. We never got past the industrial estate bit. I guess he was worried that if I turned around and said no, or I got freaked out by it, I'd go and tell somebody.'

'So, the hotel was your idea then, when you went for that?'

'Well, he suggested we go to the Tels room.'

'The what?' asked Hope.

'The telecommunications room. It's downstairs in the tower, where they do all the recordings and that. He reckoned we could go there. It's got one key. You can lock the place up, do what we do, come back out. We'd both be at work and nobody would be any of the wiser.

'You see, sometimes I have to pop downstairs, go and do a bit of admin here, there, and wherever. If there's no flights about, the air traffic controllers don't care. They're quite happy to let me do it. It wasn't a bad plan, but I wasn't getting caught having sex with him in the building. I'm not proud of what I did. You understand that, don't you? I only told your boss because you're the police and you'll keep it to yourself unless you really have to use it. But like I say, I don't think you'll need to. I don't think Curtis did anything.'

Hope stood looking out, sipping away on her coffee.

'So, the industrial estate,' said Hope, 'are there any around

159

here?'

'On the way back out of Tobermory. You'll see it on the side of the road. It's not massive. There's about six or seven units. He'll maybe have something in one of them. I don't know what, but if you go there, you should be able to find what you're looking for. To my mind, he's got to have at least one of those big wheels and knives, and it's got to be feeling like a stage to him, hasn't it? That's weird, isn't it? Real creepy.'

'Certainly sounds it,' said Hope. 'You've had a lot of adventure for being nineteen.'

'Do you have anyone?' asked Kylie. 'You haven't said it in strong tones, but you don't sound very impressed by the way I've conducted my affairs.'

'Well, it's not what I would do,' said Hope. 'I do have someone though.'

'How did you meet him?'

'Well, he was helping out with some information on a case once.'

'What's he do? Something exciting?'

'No, he's the manager of a car-hire firm.' Kylie laughed. 'Oh, it's rather dire in that sense, but he doesn't come home and tell you all about how he's hired this or what sort of people are coming into claim cars today, but he's solid, and outside of his work, he's quite exciting. Besides, I get enough wild excitement in this job. Somebody stable, sometimes it's not to be underrated, Kylie,' said Hope. 'Sorry, very condescending, wasn't it?'

'No. It's just you,' said Kylie. 'I'm me, but like I said, some of the things I've done, I'm not that proud of.'

Hope stood beside her, looking out again to the bay at Tobermory. 'But you did get a nice view from it, you really did.'

Chapter 19

With Hope away interviewing Kylie Youngs, Macleod was stuck at the airport awaiting Jona returning with further details. She had told him she'd be on her way coming back from the makeshift morgue she'd set up at the police station in Tobermory. Macleod had been pacing within the airport manager's office, but he had got sick of Curtis James watching him and so decided to take a little walk outside.

The terminal building was active, if not busy. There was still a flight to go out that evening, and as Macleod looked at the little restaurant and saw people enjoying their coffee and biscuits, awaiting the flight's arrival, he could see a normality coming back into the place. Yet, he knew he still had a killer lurking about somewhere.

He peered outside the window and on seeing there were no press about, he strode out into the cool evening. Walking along the perimeter fence, he stopped and looked down at the runway, lights shining bright, awaiting the last aircraft in. It would have been a night like this that would have been John Epson's last. *With more hail though*, he thought. He looked up at the tower, saw the dim light within and someone working.

From the shape of the person, he thought it was possibly Harold Lyme and he imagined what it must be like sitting there and looking out, watching the light of an aircraft arrive. John Epson would have been sitting, waiting, and talking to the aircraft approaching.

As he remembered, it had been quite a rough night, so there had been plenty for the controller to do. A radiotelephony replay had Epson speaking to the fire crew, and passing weather consistently out to the aircraft as well. Would he have heard anybody clanking up those twisting steps, the circular staircase that led up to the top of the tower? Maybe he wouldn't have, maybe if they did it quietly, if the killer practised it. Had they tried creeping up there? If it was one of the controllers, had it been on the back shift, last person in the building doing it?

He struggled to see how Curtis would creep up there. The man didn't appear cat-like in any shape, sense, or form. Macleod turned and watched a single light approaching the runway. As it got closer, he could see its spotlight shining down onto the runway and he watched the plane touch down with ease. It stopped, took a right, and taxied in to the main apron behind the terminal.

Pretty soon the place would be clear, security would go home, or at least, once Macleod had decided he was going home. What would he do with the airport manager for the night? Macleod was inclined to stick him in a cell; after all, he was in for questioning and at the moment, he was still a suspect. In fact, he may even be the prime suspect.

As he stood looking back out to the runway lights, he heard someone behind him, stealthy, with extremely quiet steps. Then he felt two hands on his shoulders.

'You look tense tonight, Seoras.' No one else on the team got to do this, to address him in such a way. Sure, Hope and he were on first name terms but with Jona Nakamura, Macleod had found a friend, if not quite a soulmate. They saw the world very similarly and over the years she'd known him, she had taught him how to relax, how to take in the moment, simply slip away, easing out all the anger and the frustration that the job brought. For a woman that worked with dead people, she was very good with the living.

'I think someone could do with a visit home,' said Jona.

'I thought you were just going to rub my shoulders and make it all better.'

'I don't think I'm the one to make it better. It doesn't feel like it's your head that's the problem. Do you find it harder going away?'

'Much harder than I used to,' said Macleod. 'We get on all these all-nighters and I can't cope the same way I used to. I used to keep going for forty-eight hours without sleep, not now. Take last night, the troops have been up all night but not me.'

'But they don't carry the weight of the world on their shoulders. This comes down to you; they're just the foot soldiers,' said Jona. 'I'm just a foot soldier; you're the one with the responsibility. You're not who you were twenty years ago; the body won't take it the same.'

'No, it doesn't,' said Macleod. 'Even now I am feeling tired. I need to sleep tonight.'

'They told me you sent Clarissa away.'

'I did, off carrying out investigations in Blackpool. Well, who knows what time she'll get there. She never seems to have a problem though.'

'But Clarissa doesn't carry the weight of the world on her shoulders. It's what I said. You do, all the time. You need to learn to chill out, relax, switch off.'

'We've got two dead, Jona. You can't just switch off; I've never just switched off. Even though I am sitting looking at these lights, do you know what's in my head? How? Why did he bring a plane down like this? Why had he come through here? How did he get the drugs off? How do you get in the way of someone doing that? What makes you a target for them? Over and over, it's spinning through my head. People say I'm one of the calmest people around, and I'm not. I'm just paddling like crazy underneath the surface.'

'Yes, but they don't know that,' said Jona. 'I'm the only one you tell. Well, maybe Jane as well; you don't even tell Hope that. She thinks you're some sort of serene person that just magically comes up with the ideas. 'Oh, he's got the solution because he just can see it.' You never saw anything, it's more than instinct, it's a constant churning of ideas. That mind of yours, it's not an ocean of calm; it's a tumult; it's dark and it's brooding. Sometimes you have to step away from it, Seoras.'

Macleod turned around to Jona and smiled. 'We're done when we're done. What have you got to tell me?'

Jona sucked in a deep breath of cool air. 'You're not going to like this,' she said. 'I've looked at the hands and the marks on the neck, and you can see where the indentations were. You see when you grab somebody and slit their throat, you would think that you just nick it across. Maybe you put your hand on gently just to steady yourself or to gauge the distance but not here. These knives they're using, they're not designed for that, they're designed to be thrown, to hit into a spinning wheel. They're not proper knives in that sense, so when the killers

165

had grabbed the victims by their shoulders, they've gripped tight.'

'The killers?' said Macleod. 'What do you mean, the killers?'

'Your first victim, Mr Epson, that feels like a male hand. It's big, it's thick, it's strong, real grip, but the second one, I think it's female. I think you've got two different killers.'

'Are you sure?' asked Macleod.

'The first hand is a larger hand, it's strong. It feels masculine to me. Can I say for sure it's male or female? No, I'm telling you what I'm suspecting. The second hand is daintier. I can't see a man having a hand like that.'

'See this dark tumult up in my head, Jona. You've just made it darker and it's spinning faster. I thought I was understanding it. I thought I was riding the wave. Not now. Harold Lyme can't commit this murder or Curtis. Curtis's terrible. I mean, he's an idiot. He's a sexual deviant, but he's also an idiot. I'm really struggling with that and Harold Lyme is too chilled out, too easy, laid back. I haven't got any other men it can be. That's the problem. Are you sure about this? I mean it, are you really sure?'

Jona started abruptly. 'When do I ever come to you with whimsical ideas or fancy notions? I've done my work; those are my conclusions. You put it together. You come up with it, how this is actually fitting the bill. I tell you what the bodies tell me. I tell you what the scenes of crime say to me. I tell you who's touched what, as far as I can tell. You have to tell me how it's all put together. If I had wanted to do that, I'd be a detective, not a forensic officer.'

Macleod smiled and turned back to the airfield lights. 'See that there?' he said, 'Really simple, isn't it? Just take the plane, dump it in between the lights.'

166

'Yes,' said Jona, 'make sure it's tilted slightly, so you don't put the nose into the ground. Make sure it's not tilted too much so the backside of it doesn't scrape along the ground. Also, don't tip it left and right so the wings crash. Simple as anything.'

Macleod turned and looked at her. 'It's a machine.'

'Yes, but it's also getting buffeted by something that's not mechanical, something you don't know how it reacts. Something you have to react to. When the buffet comes, sometimes you have to react quite violently.'

He stood looking out at the lights again. 'Thank you, Jona. That might be what I'm looking for. The extreme reaction, the one that goes above and beyond, the one that's coarse, maybe the forced hand.'

'If that's me, I'm heading to bed because unlike you, I was up last night.'

'Just don't switch your phone off. Keep it beside your bed, you may need it.'

'Where's Hope by the way? I was hoping to catch her for a coffee before I went to bed tonight.'

Hope and Jona had been friends for a long time and in some ways, Hope was slightly jealous when Macleod started doing his meditation classes with Jona. Still, the two women had stayed friends, even now that Hope had moved out and was with her car-hire man in Inverness.

'She's at Kylie Youngs. She wanted to chase up a lead. It's good though. It came from her. She seemed quite determined about it.'

'That's something else you could do without worrying about.'

'What?' asked Macleod.

'Seoras, she will be ready and if she isn't, somebody else will do the job. Whether you stay here or not, there will always be somebody coming up behind. Don't stay in this job for Hope's sake because you think she's not ready. Stay in this job because you want to be here, stay in it because it still gives you a reason to get out of bed in the morning. You seem to go on and on as if believing you're the only one who can think this way, the only one who can get to the bottom of these things. Hope can do it. You have to trust her a little bit more.'

'She doesn't see things the way I do. She doesn't come at it from my angle.'

'No,' said, Jona, 'and you don't come at it from her angle. That's why you work well together and the day you're gone, she will find someone who comes at it your way. That person may be young . . . or may be old. It might be a man or woman, whatever, but she will find the complement she needs. Look at you, look at what you've built around you. You can't do a paper chase. You can't trace files on a computer. You've got Ross for that, and he keeps everything ticking along because you can't keep on top of all the management duties you should have. You're no longer the Rottweiler you used to be either because you've got Clarissa. She's charging in here, there, wherever. You can set her up and off she goes, not giving a damn about whether they fire her or not, something Hope can't do. And then you've got Hope on your shoulder, chipping in from different angles, seeing the other side of things. You set that up, you made your team. That's what she'll learn from you. How to look out for herself. How to make sure that she covers all the bases by having people around her who can make up for the things she doesn't do well.'

'And what's she going to do for someone like you?'

'I'm not that old,' said Jona. 'Hope is my age. She'll have me around for a while. Now I'm getting off. I'll catch her if she makes it back to the hotel in time.'

'We're digging up things,' said Macleod, 'so don't leave your phone unattended.'

'When do I ever?'

Macleod turned, watching Jona walk back to her car, and then made the short walk back to the airport terminal. By the time he was inside, the departure lounge had cleared, everyone ready to head home after the last flight out. Those who had arrived on the plane had mostly gone as well, but Macleod crossed over to the room that Ross had camped in and found a closed door. He knocked. When it opened, Ross was standing up, and the constable apologised profusely.

'Sorry, sir, for keeping you waiting out there. Come on in. You don't have to knock, you know that.'

'Nothing wrong with politeness, Ross. Look, we're missing something here. We need to find out who came into this tower, who was on the airfield at that time at night. I need you to go back over those bases, that CCTV, who can you see? Let's see if there's any CCTV further away. See if we can track our suspects. Can we get any shots of cars on that evening, work out who we know was where, confirm they were there? Kylie Youngs, for instance, says she was in a pub. CCTV for that. Maybe they'll know her face down there. She can't even remember which one she was in.

Ross sat down. 'Yes, sir. I'll get on it.'

'Make sure you've got somebody to help you,' said Macleod. 'Grab one of the local boys or girls. Let them show you the ropes. They should know where their CCTV and everything is.'

'I haven't actually been in touch with them so far, sir. I was hoping maybe to do it tomorrow.'

169

'No,' said Macleod, 'see if you can get on it now. I just have a feeling things are going to come to a head very soon. I want to be ahead of the game.' He heard Ross sigh. 'I know. The old man's at it again, driving everyone through the night, but we need to be in front of this, Ross, and you're the man for this job.'

'Yes, sir,' he said. 'Would you do me a favour?'

'What's that?'

'The canteen's about to shut. Get them to do up a flask of coffee and leave it in here with me.'

Macleod smiled. He knew other bosses who would baulk at the idea.

'With pleasure, Ross. With pleasure.'

Chapter 20

C larissa was coming to the end of the long motorway that headed west to Blackpool, the seaside town on the northwest coast of England. Her feet were sore, her shoulders ached from all the travelling she'd just done, and frankly, she was very hacked off at Macleod. First, she'd flown out to the mainland and then hired a car to get her to Blackpool. There were younger people than Clarissa who could come down and do this. Why not Hope or even Ross? They'd be spritelier.

As the motorway ended, Clarissa slowed down to enter the town of Blackpool. She drove past a large superstore and into the carpark at the airport terminal. The lights were still on. Clarissa walked over to the sliding doors and looked around for the reception. The airport was slightly bigger than the one at Mull, but for all that, at this time of night, it was quiet. Maybe there was one more departure. The departure gates were through a door away on the far side of the building. Clarissa looked for the information desk.

'I'm sorry to bother you,' she said, 'I'm looking for Jefferson Aviation.'

'Oh, you have to go out and around to get to airside, but it'd be all closed up now. We don't normally let people through at this time of night.'

'Can you ring them? See if anyone's there.'

'I told you, we don't normally do that.'

Clarissa pulled out her identification, and held it open in front of the woman opposite her. 'You'll do it for me.' Her tone was terse. Clarissa had had enough. She'd travelled all this distance, so she wasn't going to a hotel, and then coming back in the morning. She knew that back up the road, everyone else would still be awake. Macleod chasing them around to find this and that, and just because she was in another country didn't mean she would rest on her laurels despite being sent so far away.

'You're in luck,' said the woman behind the reception desk, 'the owner, Mr Jefferson, he's actually there. He said he'll come over and pick you up. If you just wait outside, he'll be around in one of his wagons.'

'Thank you,' said Clarissa, 'what time does your airport shut?'

'Just one to go, but it's okay, Mr Jefferson gets onto his hanger by his own route. It will not stop you getting into the office.'

'Good,' said Clarissa, 'thank you for your help.' Turning on her heel, she marched out of the building, to stand waiting for Mr Jefferson. She was glad she still had her shawl on and wrapped it up tight around her, for though the night was pleasant, she was cool. Soon, a pickup truck drove up, and a man rolled down the window on the passenger side.

'Are you looking for Mr Jefferson?' he asked.

'I am, indeed.' Clarissa opened the door of the cab, stepped up into the passenger seat and produced her identification. 'Detective Sergeant Clarissa Urquhart.'

'Right. How can I help?'

'There's no need to panic,' she said, 'I need to find out about some ferry flights that you've been doing through the Isle of Mull.'

'Ferry flights to Isle of Mull? You must mean Frauke.'

'Must I?' asked Clarissa. 'Why?'

The man frowned somewhat. 'She's a quiet, young blonde girl. Good pilot. Little bit fly-by-night though. What's she done?'

'I don't know,' said Clarissa, 'I just need to know about her, if you don't mind.'

'Of course,' said the man and turned the pickup around. 'I'll take you back to the base, get you a cup of tea.'

'That's quite civil of you,' said Clarissa, warming to the man.

'Is that a Scottish accent?' he asked.

'It is. I'm based up in Inverness but working in Mull at the moment. However, the investigations have taken us down here.'

'Wow, so what? You got on the flight out of there this morning, and headed down?'

'Late afternoon, and I've driven since. I'm famished, I'm hungry, but your cup of tea sounds good.'

The man laughed, 'Well, I think we can do a bit better than that.' Once inside the small hangar that comprised Jefferson Aviation, Clarissa was taken to a canteen where a pasty was put in a microwave for her. When it came out, it looked like it had been soaked for twenty minutes, it was so droopy. However, it was hot and she soon shovelled it up, forcing it down with a wet cup of tea.

'Frauke,' said the man, 'Frauke Haas is the pilot. She goes through Mull.'

'Why?' asked Clarissa. 'Is it really ferry flights?'

'Yes, lots of them bring aircraft over from America. A lot of people get the idea they want an American aircraft, but we also do it from Europe. I mean, we'll run aircraft anywhere. It's a reasonably good business; you just have to have pilots who can adapt to small aircraft of different types, and that Frauke can do. Very competent, ready to move at any time.'

'What runs does she normally do?'

'Usually coming out of Iceland. Often, she'll take the single-engine flights that the guys won't, but she goes into Stornoway and then she pops into Mull. Personally, I think she's got somebody there. Which is fine because she doesn't hang about.'

'So, from Mull, it's straight down to here, is it?'

'Usually. Sometimes she might have to deliver an aircraft to somewhere else but most of them are coming through here for a final check before they have to get picked up'

'German name?' asked Clarissa.

'Absolutely. German completely, and she looks it. Long blonde hair. She's only twenty-five. If I were a younger man, well, who knows?' the man chortled.

Clarissa laughed again. 'You're quite a relaxed man, aren't you?' she said.

'Well, I've got nothing to hide, have I?'

'I'll find out,' said Clarissa smiling, 'but in the meantime, do you have an address for Frauke?'

'Of course. You have to send the pay somewhere, don't you? Got bank details, whatever you need.'

'Just the address is fine. How often does she fly through then? I mean, does she always stop off in Mull?'

'Sixty percent of the time, something like that. Occasionally she does fly straight down here. That's why I say I think it's a person that she wants to meet. Could be a fancy man or that.

Well, I've seen her out in the town here as well.'

'In what way?' asked Clarissa.

'Friday, Saturday nights. Oh, don't get me wrong,' said the man, 'I'm not out and about. I'll be down in the pub or just heading from one to the other, and you'll see her walking down the street off to the nightclubs. I mean she looks the part when she goes to a nightclub. Here, she's wandering around in a jumpsuit or whatever, but at the nightclub, well, she looks like she's out to party.'

'Ever any problems with her flight-wise?'

'No. Totally professional when she comes in. Never drunk, never looking like she's had any substance abuse, always on time. Nothing ever a problem. She's a great pilot for us. That's why I sort of accept the drop into Mull. We get billed for it, but she pays for it.

'She pays the landing fee,' said Clarissa. 'Is that correct?'

'Yes. I mean it gets billed to us because it's easier. Then I just deduct it out of her wages.'

Clarissa had a think. Maybe that was her way of covering up. If the company paid for it, not herself. 'Give me that address,' said Clarissa. 'I'm going to pop round tonight; please don't phone her.'

'Of course not,' said the man. 'Do you need a lift round, or anything?'

'No, my car's in the carpark. I need a lift back to it, but otherwise, I can look after myself.'

'Okay,' said the man. 'Just asking. If you do need any help, or anything else, just let me know.'

Clarissa looked up from her thoughts about Frauke and saw the man smile. At her age, she didn't think about men hitting on her, and the guy wasn't being that forthright, but he certainly seemed to like her, which was not always the case when she was out and about doing her job. She knew they called her the Rottweiler, Macleod's Rottweiler, they said at the station, but they forgot she had a more delicate side, especially in the art world where she could charm people. Sometimes she missed that side of herself.

Mr Jefferson took her back to her car, where he shook her hand firmly before lifting it up and kissing it. Clarissa could have told him off, explained how that was inappropriate as she was a police officer, but instead she smiled, stepped inside her car and saw him keeping his eyes on her as she left the carpark. If she hadn't been on a case, and not wary of the fact that she might be being played, Clarissa might have even got a number off him, some way of staying in touch.

Still, she had a job to do, and so she took the car and drove it into the centre of Blackpool. She passed all the lights along the seafront, beaming proudly for the tourists. She found a road to turn into and then looked for Frauke Haas's house. The number on the sheet was twelve, but there was no number twelve. In fact, she could only find four front doors. Getting out of the car, she went up close to each one of them and realised that there was a set of flats at the top of each.

Clarissa checked her watch. It was after ten and she could see lights on in the flats at the top of the building. Clocking the buzzer array, she saw Frauke's number, but needed to get inside to work out which flat it actually was. She pressed the buzzer of one of the other flats. When someone answered, she announced herself as the police, saying they were following up an issue about a cat. The door buzzed and she climbed up to that flat wherein the course of two minutes, she managed to explain that somebody had clearly given her the wrong address. The door closed behind and Clarissa climbed some more flights of stairs before she saw the number and the name Haas on the door.

Clarissa descended the stairs. Understanding which flat it was, from outside, she could see the lights were still on. Retiring back to her car because it was getting cold, Clarissa mused whether or not to go in, or whether to tail Frauke Haas. One of the problems she had was that there was no evidence that the woman had brought drugs in; everything was circumstantial. Yes, she was flying through, but they hadn't caught her with anything. If she simply went to talk to her, what was she meant to say? 'Oh, by the way you're bringing drugs in. Who are you handing them to? You got anything to do with that murder up in Mull?' No, she needed something—some sort of leverage.

Clarissa watched the light go out on the flat. Two minutes later, a blonde-haired woman in her mid-twenties exited the building. Clarissa saw the short skirt, the high heels, and the top that really should be worn somewhere a lot warmer. As the woman reached the end of the road, Clarissa got out of the car and began to tail her along the streets. In fairness, Clarissa felt out of place. Everywhere she looked at this time at night, there were young people heading for the nightclubs. She thought of herself probably thirty to forty years ago, making her way off to dances or discos. She could rock it in her day, but those days were long past. At the moment, she felt like a fish out of water.

Clarissa saw Frauke Haas turn into a nightclub. With two large bouncers on the door, the woman walked straight in, no hassle at all. Clarissa wondered how she was going to follow without looking decidedly overdressed, and over age. With the way the woman had walked straight into the nightclub despite the queue outside, she was clearly well known, but what did it mean?

Clarissa walked around the side of the building where she saw a door lying open at the rear. A man was sitting smoking and he was dressed in fine white shirt and black trousers. Clearly, he must have been staff. Clarissa pretended to be out of a puff, as she approached him. The man was on a beer crate turned upside down, and there was another one beside him.

'Do you mind, love,' said Clarissa. 'I'm whacked tonight.'

'Go on ahead. Not a problem.'

'Oh, and I'm busting too. Can you see that? I'm busting here. Give me a drag of that.'

The cigarette the man was smoking was taken from his hand and Clarissa took a couple of puffs before handing it back. She hated cigarettes, but she needed to get close to the man.

'Like I said, I'm absolutely busting. Can't pop in and use the toilets, can I?'

'You're not meant to come in this way. That's the staff entrance. You go around the front and ask the bouncers.'

'Oh, come on,' said Clarissa. 'Seriously, you think I'm going to look like anything, going into a nightclub, like someone's granny coming in.'

The man beside her laughed. Clarissa looked at him and saw he was still a boy. Maybe that was just her way of seeing things now. Maybe he was late teens or early twenties, one of the students working an extra job to pay for an education, who knew?

'I'm going to have to go here,' said Clarissa. 'You don't want to watch that really, do you?

The boy shook his head. 'Okay,' he said, 'if you go in, along the corridor, take a right. Don't keep going, or you'll end up towards the bar. Pop in that way, you'll see the ladies. You can make your way through from there and you won't have to go inside the club itself. Don't take the door on the left. That'll open up into the club.'

Clarissa thanked him and entered inside the building. When she got to the door, he explicitly said not to go through, she opened it, and stepped inside. Clarissa stuck to the shadows but got some rather bizarre looks from some of the people there. She remembered the clubs back in her day, but a lot of the people just seemed to be standing around. The noise was deafening, and she couldn't hear anybody. One man tapped her shoulder, and when she turned around, he started trying to wrap his leg around her leg.

'Come on, Grandma,' she heard. Clarissa put a forearm on his chest, pushed him back up against the wall. Leaning close to his ear, she said to him, 'Next time you call me Grandma, you'll walk out of here singing soprano.'

The force by which she pushed him was enough to frighten the man, and she saw his friends laughing. Clarissa moved off into the shadows again to find a dark corner to watch from, and from there she saw the dancing Frauke Haas.

There was a small handbag beside Frauke, and she watched as several men came up to dance with her, and then women as well. They came up and danced incredibly close, bodies touching, and Clarissa was quite surprised by this. She understood the idea of the sexuality that was being displayed, could understand why several men would come up and dance, and even these days why several women would join in as well. But it was for a couple of seconds that they got really close.

With a focused eye she had developed over her years as a police officer, she watched the handbag and she saw the sleight of hand. A packet was taken out and then handed over.

She was drug-dealing, thought Clarissa. She's drug-dealing here in the club. There's no wonder they let her walk in. I could just bust her now, but in the melee, I could lose her so easily. Clarissa returned to the exit she had come in, and found the man at the crate just throwing away his cigarette.

'Blimey, love. You all right?'

'Sorry,' said Clarissa. 'I got caught short and had to sit down for a bit longer than I thought but thank you.'

'Did the boss see you?'

'Not that I'm aware of. Certainly wasn't in the ladies.'

'Well, that'll be a first,' the man laughed. 'You take care. You all right to get home?'

Clarissa made a stagger then walked on up the alley. 'I'm good, son. Thank you.'

As soon as she was out of sight, Clarissa returned to her normal walk and made her way across from the exit of the club. She wondered how long she would have to wait, but she picked up the phone and called Blackpool Police Station. It was going to be a long night, but it was going to be a fruitful one.

Chapter 21

The lights of the airport terminal were still on, although security had long gone home. Leaving the airport in the hands of the police had seemed preferable to another long night. Ross was working away in one of the rooms they had taken over and Macleod still had Curtis James stuck in his office. He'd taken a phone call from Hope detailing Curtis's rather bizarre fantasy life, and the fact that he had somewhere in an industrial park that he'd asked Kylie to go to. Macleod got agitated when Hope said that Kylie didn't know where it was, but something inside him said that this was key, something that could lead them on to discover what was really happening. They'd need to know where it was, though.

Macleod opened the door of the airport manager's office and slammed it shut behind him. Curtis James looked up from his desk and Macleod stared at him.

'You asked Kylie Youngs to go to an industrial park to take part in some sort of little fantasy, correct?'

The man shook. Macleod could see him begin to sweat.

'No, I did nothing of the sort.'

'Why is she lying to me? You've already asked her for sex to give her a job. Was this for promotion? How does this work?

Is this what you really wanted? You didn't get played by a nineteen-year-old, did you?'

Macleod saw the rage in the man's eyes, and then he seemed to quiet down.

'I didn't get played by anybody and I didn't give her sex.'

'She said you wanted to take her down to the Tels room as well, initially, to get her on her own. Is that what you like, them on their own? Sarah Pullet was on her own.'

Curtis looked up. 'I didn't do anything with Sarah.'

'So, you did with Kylie?'

'There's no industrial estate, this is all fabrication. It's all lies.'

Macleod sat down in the chair opposite and stared intently at the man. He was sweating like crazy. Macleod could see the armpits becoming drenched. In all his years as a police officer, he'd seen those who couldn't lie. They were sure they were calm enough, but their stories were never straight. There were those who could lie perfectly, very hard to recognise what they were doing. Curtis James was someone who couldn't lie at all, but worse than that, gave away every clue that he was lying by his body breaking out almost in a fever.

'So, you're telling me there's not been an industrial estate?'

'No, never,' said the man.

'You're telling me you never wanted to be like your uncle.'

'Oh, I've wanted to be like him in one sense, but not like that. On a proper stage.'

'You never wanted to be him in a sort of little fantasy with some young girl.'

Curtis looked away desperately, then looked down towards his feet, then he raised his head up again. 'No, never. I'd never do that. Ellie wouldn't go for something like that.'

'Ellie wouldn't go for you entertaining a young woman in that fashion or Ellie wouldn't do that herself?'

'She wouldn't go for the . . .' Curtis seemed to think. Macleod knew that the man was struggling to keep his story straight. It was the case that she wouldn't agree with him running off with a young woman, but neither did Macleod think that she would entertain Curtis's desires either. The man threw his arms on the desk, put his head down, and started to cry. Macleod stood up, walked back out of the room, and picked up his mobile phone.

'This is Hope.'

'Hope, Seoras, I want you to go to the industrial park, get it searched. The guy's lying through his teeth, but he's not going to come clean. He's almost in denial about what he's done. I think we have got a raging pervert here, but I'm not convinced that he's in any shape, sense, or form, a killer, but we need to find this location in the industrial park. Maybe it will tell us something.'

'I'll get on it, sir,' said Hope. 'Have you had any word from Clarissa?'

'None,' said Macleod. 'Ross is still checking all the CCTVs as well. I'm just getting the feeling we need to move soon.'

'Why?' asked Hope. 'What's up?'

Macleod spun round within the airport terminal. Quiet as it was, he wanted to make sure no one was listening. 'It's just that if someone's selling Curtis out, if he's meant to be the fall guy and we don't look like we're buying it, at some point, they're going to run, and if they run, we may not catch them. There are too many people at the moment to put a net around to prevent them from running away. We need to get on with this, and we need to hold Curtis. It'll make it look like he's our main suspect and not that we can see through it.'

'That's understood. We'll keep that between you and me then and the rest of the team,' said Hope. 'Jona as well. Put the other officers on it, but not let them know that side of it in case it gets out.'

'Agreed,' said Macleod. 'Go find me what's on that industrial estate.'

He put the phone down, turned around, and walked back into the office and took up his seat opposite Curtis James again.

'You can talk anytime you want,' he said. 'Just be aware we are searching the industrial park, so anytime you want to come clean, I'm right here.' Curtis looked up and Macleod stared at him. The armpits weren't getting any drier.

* * *

Hope waved down the security guard as he arrived in his car. The man looked somewhat flustered as she walked over to him. When she climbed inside his car, he looked somewhat sheepish.

'Sorry to get you out this time of night; are you all right?' asked Hope.

'I wasn't expecting to come out, sorry,' he said. Hope could smell the alcohol on his breath.

'How many have you had?'

'Just a couple. It's all right, I'm sensible and it won't be a problem. It's just we're not meant to when we're on call.'

'Well, I'm not here to bust you,' said Hope. 'I just need your help. This industrial estate, what have we got on it? I mean, who owns these different places?'

'Well, that one's operating fish out of there. It's a unit where they gut and clean them and take them out. One across from it, that's a craft place. There are two storage warehouses. I think they're sending things off around the globe. The next one, that's a charity hub.'

'Is that it?' asked Hope.

'No, some of them sublet some of the land. There's a couple of containers, you know, like shipping containers around the other side of that building.'

'Can you take me to those?'

'Of course.'

The man stepped out of the car followed by Hope, and together they walked across the dark forecourt before arriving at shipping containers on the far side of one of the buildings. Hope could see three and pointed to the first one.

'What's in that?' she asked.

'Old equipment storage from the fish people.'

'That one?'

'That's the charity people. They sometimes store stuff in that. I'm not sure if it's empty. Hang on.' He walked up and pulled open the large heavy door at the front of the container.

'They just leave it open?' said Hope.

The man pulled a flashlight out, shone it inside. 'Look,' he said, 'there's nothing in there; that's why it's open. That's why I was checking. If they have stuff, they lock it.'

'Okay,' said Hope. 'What about this one?'

'Been like that a while. I think it's owned by the airport.'

'Really? What do they store in there?'

'Never seen anything in there. It does have electricity running to it. It's been there for a number of years now. When it got put in, I remember seeing it. They touched it up, but there was nothing inside, and then one day, it got locked up.

You can see the large padlock in the front. I don't have the code to that, I'm sorry. I'm not privy to what's inside. I'm here to secure the premises, not the contents.'

'That's understood,' said Hope, and approached the lock. It had four digits on it. Then she thought about getting some bolt croppers to cut it, but instead, she phoned Macleod.

'Seoras, I've got a container that's owned by the airport. Do you want to ask Curtis what it's for?'

Macleod looked up at Curtis James across the table from him. 'Mr James, I've got my sergeant currently staring at a container on the industrial estate just outside Tobermory. Apparently, it's owned by the airport. What's in there?'

'Don't know,' he said.

'You don't know? Who do I phone to find out?' asked Macleod.

'Oh, you don't,' said Curtis. 'You don't need to talk to head office.'

'Is that because head office don't know about it?' Curtis stared at him. 'It's got a padlock on it,' said Macleod. 'You don't think you could provide us with the code for that padlock? Four digits, apparently.'

Curtis looked at him and then looked away.

Macleod picked up the phone. 'He's not being very cooperative, Hope.'

'Not surprising,' she said. 'Tell you what, though, I mean, he's not the cleverest, is he? What's his date of birth?'

Macleod looked over at the man. 'When were you born?' he said.

Curtis stared at him.

'It's not a difficult question,' said Macleod. 'When were you born? What was the date when you were born?' When he didn't respond, Macleod strode out of the office over to Ross. 'Sorry to bother you,' he said, 'I need to know the date of birth of Curtis James. I take it you've got the personnel records here.'

Ross paused the CCTV he was looking at. 'Yes, I have, sir, just a second. There you go, 4th of the 5th, '65. 4th of the 5th, '65.'

'Excellent,' said Macleod. He put the phone up to his ear. 'You get that, Hope? 4th of the 5th, '65.'

Hope looked down at the padlock, put a four, and then a five, and then a six and a five into it, and pulled hard. The padlock didn't move.

'That's not right,' said Hope. 'Just a second. I'll see if he's put it in back to front,' she put a 5, then a 4, then a 65.

'No, it's not right either,' she said.

'Well, just get a set of bolt croppers or something. Get through the lock and get that open.'

'Just a second, sir,' said Hope. She looked down and put a one, then a nine in, then a six, and a five. She pulled and the metal curved bar at the top of the padlock shifted up allowing her to free up the lock.

'He really is a simple soul, Seoras. It's 1965, doesn't even have any of the other stuff in it.'

'Well, what do you see?'

'Hang on, I've got to get inside first.'

With the assistance of the security guard, Hope pulled open the front doors of the container. The security guard stepped inside and fumbled before finding a switch and flicked it on. Inside, Hope saw what looked like a mini circus setup. At the centre of it was a large wheel which could be spun. It had a number of knives sticking out of it. She could see the binds where a person would be held. What was bothering her was the fact that there were pictures of a crowd attached to the doors that they'd just opened as if people were sitting watching this.

'You're not going to believe this, Seoras,' she said.

'Why? What can you see?' Hope switched on the phone's video and fed the stream through to Macleod's phone. He marched into the office and placed the phone in front of Curtis James.

'Do you want to explain this one?' he said. 'You told me you never wanted to take Kylie Youngs to a container, and yet look, it's set up just like your thing at home. You need to start talking, Mr James.'

'Just a moment,' said Hope. Taking a glove out of her back pocket, she removed one of the knives, placed it down under the lights, and took a photograph of it. She hung up the call to Macleod and rang Jona instead. She quickly advised her of the situation and sent an image of the knife.

'You better call the boss,' said Jona. Hope dialled Macleod into the call as well so the three of them were able to see each other.

'So, what's the big deal?' asked Macleod. 'What else have you found?'

'A knife, sir,' said Hope. 'I took a photograph of it, passed it to Jona.'

'Inspector, I can't say for definite, well, being a true professional, I won't say for definite until I get it in my hands, but from the photograph, that knife is not like the ones he had up in his house. That knife is a match for the ones that slit the throats of our two victims.'

'Bingo,' said Macleod. 'Do you realise what this means?'

188

'What, that Curtis actually did do it?' said Hope.

'We've been right all along. Somebody has set him up so good.'

'This was his, he would've…,' and Hope stopped.

'Yes,' said Macleod. 'Somebody would've had to been taken in there by him. Somebody would have to know that Curtis entertained in that fashion.'

Chapter 22

The sergeant at Blackpool Police Station had taken a little convincing to get a raid together for Frauke Haas's apartment. He was quite happy that Clarissa had spotted her dealing drugs in the nightclub, but he wanted to make an arrest on her there rather than wait for her to leave. His fear was that she wouldn't have any drugs on her at that point, and maybe the house was empty.

But Clarissa had a feeling that there would be plenty stored up there. More than that, Clarissa wanted to get into the house to see if she could find any other connections to Iceland, and to see how the drugs were being brought in, and from whom? It had taken another hour of conversation with the sergeant before he left one of his officers in plain clothes outside the club waiting for Haas to come out while Clarissa was taken to the station, and they talked through a plan. The watching officer then called to say that Haas was leaving, and by the time Clarissa got back into her car and arrived back at the flat, the woman had entered, along with a young man.

Clarissa was sitting in the back of an unmarked van in the street at Haas's flat and looking across at six officers who were going to approach the house and arrest her. The duty sergeant had suggested that they take down six officers because of the man who had gone into the house with her. He didn't fancy there being any ruckus and believed the show of strength would be enough to contain them.

He advised Clarissa not to join them, rather to wait, and this was something she took real offence at. Maybe it was because she was dressed in her boots, rather bright, garish trousers, and shawl that made people think she wasn't anything but an eccentric woman. But Clarissa could teach these people a few things. However, she was out of her patch, and she needed their cooperation, so she swallowed her pride and just let them get on with it.

As the doors opened from the back of the van, she watched the six officers get out and make their way over to the front door of the flat, where they opened it and climb up the stairs. Clarissa stood outside, and she could see a light coming on as the officers reached the top.

Standing beside the van, Clarissa looked up and saw the curtains fly open from one of the windows. She saw Frauke Haas pulling on a t-shirt, shouting something at someone behind her. The team that were there to arrest her had assumed it'd just be simple, open the door, move in, and bring them out, but Clarissa was beginning to have second thoughts about that. They were knocking on the door, and Haas was simply getting dressed and looking for her escape route, looking to see if anyone was down here. All she would see was an older woman with her bright-coloured trousers and her shawl.

Clarissa left the van and walked over to one of the other sets of flats and found an alley leading down to the rear of it. When it arrived at the rear of the set of flats that Haas was in, Clarissa could see the fire escape, a set of winding metal staircases. Running down the escape were Haas and her man.

'Police! Stop!'

The man turned around and looked at Clarissa. 'You're having a laugh, love,' he said.

'Do her,' said Haas and ran off into the back alley. The man jumped down off the last step and came running towards Clarissa. She was not one to get into a fight, but generally, she fought dirty, so she was glad that the man was coming at her at pace.

Clarissa stood her ground. As he got closer, she could see the man winding up his fist, pulling it back to try and strike her on the jaw. As he arrived, he made a swing. Clarissa stepped to one side. The man overbalanced, and she kicked him hard in the shins as he hurtled past. This caused him to fall to the ground. As he did so, Clarissa kicked him hard three times. She then pushed him onto his back, took out her handcuffs, and put them around each wrist. She could hear people coming down the fire escape now, and she looked up to see the officers who had been sent up to arrest the couple.

'She's fled that way,' said Clarissa. 'One of you, pick up this guy.'

Clarissa stood and watched the bulk of the team head up the alleyway. As they sprinted off, Clarissa pulled out her phone, pulling up a map of Blackpool. She closed the screen in onto Haas's flat and looked at the streets around.

Where would you go? she thought. *It's the early hours of the morning, so a lot of people are going to be off the street. You'd need to go somewhere to get away. Somewhere where they wouldn't look for you.*

Clarissa turned on her heel, walked off back down the alleyway, and strode out to the sea front. She looked along to see where it was still open. A lot of the nightclubs were empty, but there were other places, a few adult entertainment spots that were still reasonably lively.

If you went looking for a woman, the last place you'd be looking is inside one of the gentleman's clubs, she thought. *Maybe the girl even had contacts in there. She could move back to the nightclub, of course. She'd certainly have contacts in there.*

It was going to be difficult. She wondered if the others would catch up with Haas first but Clarissa walked along to the nightclub where she saw two bouncers still on the door. The wide doors behind them, however, were opened, and it seemed that the nightclub had closed.

Clarissa stood on the wall at the Blackpool seafront, staring at the open club doors. She was there for at least five minutes before a figure, now dressed in jeans and a t-shirt, made its way up to the bouncers. She saw the long blonde hair, and the smile from them, allowing Haas to enter the club. She picked up her phone and dialled the sergeant who had run the extraction team looking to arrest.

'This is Sergeant Urquhart. I take it you're having no luck.'

'She's gone. I'm sorry, she's gone. We didn't realise there was that route out the back.'

'No, you didn't,' said Clarissa, 'but you're in luck because I've found her. Back to the club,' she said. 'She's gone back inside, just walked past two of the bouncers.'

'We have her then,' he said. 'We'll come up and we'll make a raid on the club, find her in there.'

'You do that,' said Clarissa. 'I'll just keep my distance, stay nice and safe.'

'Yes, it could get rough in there, Sergeant. Probably best if we handle it.'

'Probably best,' said Clarissa. She looked across at the bouncers and crossed over the road, and down to the alley that led to the rear of the club, back to where she'd been sitting, taking the drag from the bartender's cigarette. When she got there, she saw the door was still open.

Clarissa pulled over at one of the crates and took a seat. It would take the officers at least, what, five minutes to get there? There'd be a bit of commotion, so yes, she would have time. As Clarissa sat there, the same young man she'd spoken to that night came out with a new cigarette in his mouth, puffing away.

'It's you,' he said. 'I thought you would have gone home.'

'No, I needed to come back but it's okay, not for you.'

The man laughed. 'You look a lot more sober than you did before.'

'I'm totally sober,' said Clarissa. 'I'm just going to sit near the door until someone comes out.'

'Well, I've come out,' he said.

'Nope, I'm not looking for you. Are you aware that drugs are dealt in that club?' said Clarissa.

'Really? I kind of guessed it. I mean, dealt at a lot of clubs, aren't they? Must be hard for them to stop it. They have their bouncers at the door to try and prevent things like that.'

'Bouncers who let that happen. Or maybe they're letting the right people in to deal their drugs,' said Clarissa. 'I guess they wouldn't want other people from other patches or gangs, whatever it is you have down here in Blackpool.'

'You're not from here?' asked the man, pulling up the crate beside Clarissa.

'No,' she said. 'Not at all. Work out of Inverness.'

'Well, you've got the right accent for it,' the man said. 'It must be something big if you're down here this time of night. A long way from Inverness.'

'Yes,' said Clarissa. 'Long way.'

'I take it you're a police officer then,' said the man.

'Detective Sergeant Clarissa Urquhart,' she said, 'at your service.'

'And you're just sitting here?' said the man. 'Seems a bit bizarre. I thought you'd be going in and arresting someone.'

'No,' said Clarissa. 'They'll be coming out here to me in a minute.'

'How do you know?'

'Experience,' she said. 'The key to catching someone isn't being faster than them. It isn't being stronger than them. The key is actually being ahead of them, being ready for them. You don't have to be a superhero. You don't have to charge around. You just have to bide your time, pick your right moment, and when it comes, you have to be brutal in your execution, because quite often they'll be bigger or stronger than you.'

'Really?' said the man. 'It's not the way they do it on TV.'

'Well, no, but we don't have that many people touching sixty running around on TV, do we?'

'I thought you were a lot older than me. Sorry, I thought you could be my granny.'

'Well, coming from somebody of your age, I guess that's fair enough,' said Clarissa. 'Listen,' she said, 'can you hear that?'

'Oh, sounds like someone's kicking off at the front.'

'That's the police squad about to move in and grab who we're looking for. The bouncers will have been putting up a fight against them because they won't want her to be caught because she's got drugs on her. Or at least supplies drugs in here.'

'Wow,' said the man. 'So, what? You're going to do what

195

now?'

'I'm just going to move this crate out of the way, and you're going to need to move.'

'Right. Where do you want me to go?'

Clarissa pointed over from the door. 'Just go over there and sit down.'

'Do you want me to help at all?' asked the man.

'No, you'd probably lose your job, and secondly, you'd probably get hurt, so no. Best if I do this.' The man nodded, sat down, but from inside the club, they could hear shouts and yells.

'Do you want a drag off a cigarette before she gets here?'

'I don't smoke,' said Clarissa. 'I just did that earlier on to get inside the club.'

'Wow,' the man said. 'So, what, you played me to get inside the club?'

'Well, they wouldn't let me in the front door, would they? Look at me. Like you said, it would be your granny turning up. Oh, hang on,' said Clarissa.

'What?' said the man.

'Footsteps, just a moment.' Clarissa moved over to the door which was sitting open. The footsteps got louder until suddenly, Clarissa shoved the door hard. It hit something coming out the door and then it swung back open. Clarissa looked around at the prone body on the floor.

'Wow, you caught her, all right.'

But Clarissa wasn't listening. She bent down on one knee, spun the blonde-haired girl over, and secured her with a plastic tie because her handcuffs had already been used. She had a number of plastic ties just in case.

As Clarissa stood back up, two police officers arrived and

looked down at the floor. 'Can you get her back to the station, guys?' said Clarissa. 'I'll follow you presently.' The men pulled her up to her feet, took an arm each, but as they walked away, Clarissa asked them to stop.

'We should just do this here,' she said, and she patted down the trousers of Haas, who looked at her with venom. There was blood running down from the side of her nose but Clarissa ignored it, instead reaching inside the pockets of her trousers. From one, she took a couple of bags of a white powder and handed them to one of the constables.

'Take that with you. Make sure it gets signed in.' From the other pocket, Clarissa, with a gloved hand, took out a mobile phone. She pressed it on but realised it was locked out. However, over the front of the locked-out screen were some messages, one of which was a text conversation. It had the answer, 'Okay.' Above it was one word that had been sent to whoever it was on the other end of the line.

'Ragnarök,' said Clarissa. 'Really? Ragnarök?'

As the officers took Frauke Haas away to the police station, the young man stood up beside Clarissa.

'Ragnarök? It's all very dramatic, isn't it?' he said.

'The end,' said Clarissa. 'It's going to be a long night,' she said, 'but just not down here.'

Chapter 23

We're doing this officially now, Mr James. That's why we're in this room, that's why there's a tape running. This is no longer inquiries. What we have is your container, containing knives that are identical to those that were used in the murder of John Epson and also of Sarah Pullet. Given that the knives matched those that were used and given that these knives are in a lockup that you organised, I would say you have some explaining to do, and I want the explanation to come fast.'

'But I didn't kill anyone. I never killed anyone,' said Curtis James. He got up from his seat and started to pace the room, sweat pouring off his face, which had gone red in anger and frustration.

'Then, tell me about it,' said Macleod. 'Tell me right now exactly what you have done, because you've been lying to me from the start. You've tried to hide every sort of detail of what you do.'

'Of course, I did. Look at me, just look at me. Don't get me wrong, Inspector. I'm a lech, and I'm a mess as well. Yes, Kylie Youngs put it on a plate, told me I could have her, and all she needed was a job. I bought it, and I thought, "Yes, this will be the start, and I'll be able to keep her as some side piece," but she played me, like I always get played. We had one time, one time, and it wasn't even doing what I wanted to do. Yes, I love the circus; yes, I love the knife act; and yes, I have dreams, fantasies about what to do. Yes, I was stupid enough to actually write them down.'

Hope was standing behind Macleod; she nodded. 'That really was stupid. How safe is your safe?'

'What do you mean?' asked Curtis James.

'I mean how safe is your safe?' said Hope. 'Has anybody else seen that diary? Did anybody else know what was in it? Was it ever out of the safe when you were out of the room?'

'Of course not. You don't leave something like that lying around, do you?' said James.

'Was your combination for the safe as difficult as the combination for the lockup?' said Hope.

Curtis James went red in the face, turned around and started swearing to the wall.

'Oh, my goodness,' said Hope.

'What?' asked Macleod.

'It's the same. It's just his date of birth.'

'I'm afraid you're not the sharpest tool in the box, are you, Mr James? If I was you, I'd speak very quickly about what's been going on.'

'I have no idea if anybody read that diary,' he said. 'Absolutely no idea. They laugh at me around here, you know that. I go over with my ideas for the airport, and they just tell me it can't be done. That's not how management works, you have to push the boundaries. You have to drive forward ideas that people don't find feasible at first, but they find a way to make it work.'

'I'm not sure that's how air traffic would see it,' said Macleod, 'or indeed anybody with their safety hat on in the aviation industry. Maybe you would've been wiser to not come up with such fanciful ideas, but enough about that. Why are you telling me about this?'

'Because I'm the boss; I'm in charge. I'm the one who needs respect around here.'

'You have a funny way of imposing respect on women,' said Hope. 'You know that women can actually respect a man without being attracted to them?'

Curtis looked incredulously at Hope, but even through that, she could still see his mind working in the background. 'You really have got a problem with women, don't you?' said Hope.

'I think you're right, Sergeant,' said Macleod. 'I think one of the women here realised that and played you. I don't mean Kylie Youngs.'

'She's just a girl. Sharp-minded, but a girl,' said Curtis. 'Played me well, and I barely got near her. I wanted something long-term with her, but it didn't happen.'

'Okay then,' said Macleod. 'Who else? Somebody else played you, somebody else got in under your skin. Somebody.'

'Was just the once as well.'

'Who?' asked Macleod.

'It was on an away day. We had a day out, at one of those hotels and she came up to me, and we were meant to be sharing about things we'd enjoyed in childhood. She talked about the circus. I love the circus. It's, it's everything to me, outside of here. Ellie doesn't understand. Doesn't understand what it means to be up the front. Doesn't understand what it means to have the adoration.'

'Especially women,' said Hope.

'Exactly,' said Curtis. 'Especially the women.'

Macleod rolled his eyes, looked over at Hope, but he gave her a smile, too, because she was spot on. The way the man was, was the way the man was. Hope and he had got through, had begun to understand it.

'She says to me about enjoying the circus,' said Curtis. 'I said to her that I was into all that. I really enjoyed the knife throwing. In fact, I'd been trained in the knife throwing. She said, 'Okay. Where could we do this knife throwing?' I said to her that my wife was a jealous kind, so we'd have to do it on the quiet.'

'Did you have the lockup at this point?' said Hope.

'It has been there for a year or so.'

'Why?' asked Hope.

'Because that's where Mr James goes,' said Macleod, 'isn't it? You go, and you stand there, and you have all the faces looking back at you, and you act out your fantasies there. You're throwing knives in an empty wall, but you wanted somebody real on there, and then for everything to fall into place.'

'Well, I took her,' he said, 'and she was there, up on the wheel. I spun the wheel, I threw knives and then afterwards, I tried to get a little bit more romantic.'

'That's what you call it,' said Hope. Macleod waved his hand indicating she shouldn't speak because he wanted Curtis to continue.

'That was romantic, but she didn't fall for it. Came back here and just carried on with the job until a month ago.'

'What happened then?' asked Macleod. Curtis started to shake. 'I said, what happened then?'

'She said she was ready, and we came, and we did the knife-throwing again, but this time, afterwards, she responded, and

201

we, well, we lived out that fantasy. The one you've read in the book,' said Curtis crossly at Hope. 'It was amazing. Absolutely amazing. I couldn't believe it was her either. She's so strong, so dominant, yet she collapsed in my arms. She was just like putty.'

'I'm not sure she was the putty here,' said Hope.

'How many times did this happen?' asked Macleod.

'Once. Once and then she came into my office the next day and she said to me, if I told anyone, she'd come for me. Said, I couldn't reveal it.'

'You're scared of her, aren't you? said Macleod. 'You're really scared of her.'

'She's so determined, quite fierce. She can take on all the men.'

'Who?' asked Hope, 'who?'

'Julia Fluke,' said Macleod. 'She's the strong female controller here. She's the one who stands up to you. Did you know any of the knives were missing?'

'Of course not,' said Curtis. 'I didn't, I haven't been back in there since. I was scared, scared she'd have people watching because she told me not to go back, told me to leave it alone for months.'

'Why didn't you mention this before?' said Hope.

'With all this heat on, with people being murdered, you don't know what way you people will read it.'

'Yet, she was doing you up like a kipper,' said Macleod. 'Slowly, bit by bit. She knew we'd get there. She realised how daft you were, keeping that diary in the safe. The lockup. Then when you went there, you'd say, 'Oh no, this is what Julia did,' but you'd already turned around and said that you hadn't even been with Kylie Youngs. You lied the whole way along.

202

She knew you would. She knew the type of person you were,' said Macleod. 'Person throwing everybody else under the bus to save their own skin. She also knew what it would sound like. I take it nobody else witnessed your antics with her.'

'No,' said Curtis.

'You left yourself exposed,' said Hope. She looked at her watch. 'Just coming around to five in the morning, sir. We need to act on this. We might be able to catch her while she's still in bed.'

'Good idea,' said Macleod. 'Go get Ross, and together start organising a party to go and grab her.'

Macleod watched Hope leave the room. His mind was easier as he knew what had happened. But he also knew this was the end game, when you had to grab the people before they ran, before they were away. He needed to keep everything quiet. There was no trust that Curtis wouldn't blab his mouth.

'Mr James, we're going to keep you in the cells for your own protection,' said Macleod. It was probably a half-truth. 'Of course, you're entitled to a lawyer.'

'For what? Do you still not believe me?'

'It's not a case of believing. We have to prove it. Do you have any idea why Julia Fluke was treating you in this way other than to put you up for murder? Do you know why she killed Mr Epson or Sarah Pullett?'

'No,' said Curtis.

'Have you ever known Miss Fluke to use drugs?'

'No. I mean, they get medicals and stuff in that, and it's the controllers.'

'Have you ever seen her with any drugs?'

'No,' he said.

'There's been a problem with drugs on the island,' said

Macleod. 'For what it's worth, I reckon that they were getting dropped in here by plane. The pilot was coming across to use the toilets, then Julia Fluke was picking up the goods from there and taking them home. There was no security to pick any of it up.'

'But that's crazy,' said Curtis. 'We had the sniffer dogs here. They were in the terminal. They went to the lower apron. They were around aircraft coming in.'

'If you work in the tower, you can look down on that apron. You can see where and when the police are there with the dogs. Simple phone call, simple text message to someone flying along. If we go back and check the records, I think you'll see there's been a few diversions, on the occasions they would've run into trouble.'

Macleod's phone beeped. He reached down, and picked it up. There was a message from Clarissa. On reading it, he rang her instantly.

'Just fill me in again,' said Macleod.

'Basically, one of the pilots always came through Mull with ferry traffic, bringing a different plane each time, Iceland to Stornoway, down to Mull and then on to Blackpool. When I tailed her here, I found she'd been dealing. She tried to run, but we caught her. The only thing was that she saw us coming. She just texted a message on her phone, saying Ragnarök.'

'Ragnarök? Like with the Norse legends?'

'Exactly, Seoras,' said Clarissa. 'End time. End of everything. I think it's a signal to run.'

'Did you get the number it was sent to?'

'Of course,' said Clarissa. 'Here,' and she rhymed off the number on the phone.

Macleod stood up and walked out of the interview room.

He barged through into one of the offices where Hope was talking to Ross.

'Contact details. Contact details,' said Macleod.

'For whom?' asked Ross.

'The controllers,' said Macleod. 'Here. This number, whose number is this?'

Ross took the number, jumped in front of his computer, and started looking up the personnel records he had for the staff at the airfield.

'Julia Fluke's mobile.'

'Where did you get that number from, sir?' asked Hope.

'Clarissa's found the drug dealer at the other end, but they said they had to catch her after she tried to run. She texted this message through.'

'Why would she text it to Julia Fluke's phone?' asked Ross.

'She texted Ragnarök. It's all over. They're running. She's not going to text to a SIM card that might get seen in a day or two. She has to go direct for the main number because this is an emergency. Hope, get around to Julia Fluke's now. Ross, go with her. Hurry.'

Chapter 24

Hope tore out of the car park, causing Ross to sit tight in his seat. She drove at breakneck speed around corners. On approaching the house, Hope realised that all the lights were out and there was no car in the drive. Jumping out, she ran up the driveway and began looking in the windows.

'No one there,' said Ross, looking in behind her.

'Don't be so sure. Come on, let's check around the back of the house as well.' Together, they strode along the edge of the house, passing some well-maintained border gardens on their way to the rear. Hope tried the door and found that it opened.

'Left in a hurry, then,' said Ross.

'If she left at all,' said Hope. She edged inside, entering into the kitchen. Hope touched the kettle and some pans that were sitting on the stove, but none of them were hot. She opened the fridge and saw that it was half-full. Carefully, the pair crept through the house and began to climb the stairs. As they neared the top, Hope thought she heard a creak. She ducked down, peering around the corner of the banister as best she could.

'Might just be the wind creaking,' whispered Hope.

'I certainly hope so.'

Ross moved past her but flanked her again when she then walked past him again. They opened each bedroom door but found no one inside. Hope looked at the main bedroom and pulled back all the drawers in the unit beside the bed. It looked like half the clothes were missing and they'd been pulled out in a hurry.

'Looks like she's gone.'

Together they went back downstairs, but Hope saw a flashing light, this time on the answering machine. Hope pressed the button.

'Jules, this is Zoe. I can't believe it's happened. Okay, it's time to go. I agree with you. I'll see you at the ferry. Once we get over to the other side we can head off, catch a plane to somewhere, or take a boat. I'll bring the money with me. There should be enough here to keep us comfortable for years to come. See you there. I love you.'

There was a beep that finished the call. Hope looked at Ross.

'The ferry,' he said. 'We need to get to the ferry.'

Hope nodded and went to run back down the hallway to the rear door. She stopped in her tracks and looked at the picture on the wall. It was Zoe and Julia together. Hope looked at the two of them and realised that they weren't just good friends, there was something more there. At least certainly from Zoe's face.

Hope ran out of the rear door and into the car, starting it before Ross had climbed in beside her.

'You phone Macleod. I'll get down to the ferry; we'll meet him down there.'

As Hope tore away from the house, she could see the dawn rising, light beginning to permeate through the darkness. It will be an early morning ferry. Macleod will call it through, get people down there as soon as possible. Then again, given the ferry's location, far away from Tobermory, maybe they were the nearest officers, especially as they were en route.

'Sir,' said Ross, in the seat beside Hope. 'It's Julia Fluke; she's done a runner. We believe Zoe Jillings is also involved. You could send someone round there, but we believe they've gone on the run and they're going to meet up at the ferry.'

'Two people involved,' said Macleod on the phone. 'That's our two people. Zoe Jillings was in on the day of Epson's death. If they're running, they'll have taken their drug money with them; that's what they were talking about. Julia Fluke set this all up; she's the brain box. She thought about what had happened with Curtis. Go, Ross, go. I'm following you down now.'

Ross closed the call and looked over at Hope. 'We'll probably be first there. Let's hope we're on time; it's an early ferry this morning.'

As they drove along the main road toward the ferry, Hope could see that there was a reasonable amount of traffic on the road. Clearly, the early ferry was popular. As she neared the slipway, she found the traffic getting bogged down. Hope pulled over to one side near the terminal and walked up to the information desk inside.

She pulled out her badge and stuck it in the face of the receptionist. 'I'm Detective Sergeant Hope McGrath; who's in charge of the ferry?'

'Well, the master. He's on the ferry.'

'Who's in charge of the terminal?'

'Mr Anderson. He won't be in at the moment. He usually comes in for later sailings.'

'Who's in charge now?' said Hope, raising her tone some-what.

'June. Hang on a minute. June,' the woman shouted over behind her. An older woman with blonde hair that was neatly permed strode over in a crisp white shirt.

'Can I help you?'

'These are detectives,' said the woman behind the counter.

'Detective Sergeant Hope McGrath, we need to stop the ferry from departing. We need to contain everyone arriving at the moment. I've potentially got two suspects about to go on.'

'Okay. Are they dangerous?' she asked.

'Potentially so,' said Hope. 'I'm going to need your assistance. Can you get me a line to the captain?'

The woman nodded, and Hope pointed to Ross. 'Get on to the master; tell him he doesn't move and not to let down the ramp.'

Ross nodded and took the phone off the woman. She turned back to Hope, 'What else can we do for you?'

'We need to corral the cars in, but I don't want any indication that anything is wrong. I want them all to come in and get set up to go on to the boat. Then, we need to block off the rear so they can't go anywhere.'

'That shouldn't be a problem,' said the woman. 'We'll just let them come in as normal.'

'To block them off?'

'Put a couple of vehicles behind the queue when you're ready for it. If they're coming in a car, they're going to be in the middle of the queue anyway, there's nowhere to go.'

Hope nodded and informed the woman that she wanted a couple of vehicles to be standing by ready to close off the queue at her command. Stepping outside of the building and looking over towards the queue, Hope scanned up and down, but she couldn't see Julia Fluke or Zoe Jillings anywhere amongst the cars. Maybe they'd disguised themselves. She looked over towards the rear end of the queue and saw another squad car coming down.

She picked up her mobile, calling Macleod.

'Seoras, it's Hope. We've got containment down here. I need you not to come in with all squad cars. It'll just spook them at the moment. I'm trying to get them to believe that nothing's gone wrong.'

Hope saw the squad car turn around and start driving the other way.

'Understood. I'm on that one,' said Macleod. 'I'll jump out and come down towards you.'

Hope wasn't too sure that was a good idea either, but this was the boss. He wanted to be down overseeing what was happening. She stood just beside the front door of the terminal seeing Macleod approach and stepping lightly past several cars before reaching her.

'Do we know they're in that queue?' asked Macleod.

'No idea. We've contacted the ferry. They're not going to drop the ramp. I'm going to get a couple of cars to close off the rear of the queue. Then we'll start searching through, but I wanted to do it quietly. Not with uniform in case they see us coming.'

'Good,' said Macleod. 'We both know what Julia Fluke looks like. Let's make our way up. Zoe Jillings as well. They might be in disguise.'

'I had thought about that,' said Hope. 'I think it best, if we take a quick run-up, first of all, then we can search car by car, if we haven't found them initially.'

'Good idea,' said Macleod. The pair of them walked over towards the front car and were joined by Ross.

'Just walk up in between nice and slowly. Keep your eyes and ears open. If you see anything, holler,' said Macleod. Together, the three detectives walked up the two lines checking the line of cars. There were two lines side by side, ready to go on the ferry. With some forty cars, Macleod made his way forward, walking in the middle, looking in at either side. As he got halfway up the line, he noticed a woman looking at him. She had a scarf around her head and some heavy makeup on, but he could see the shock in her face.

'Hope, Ross, green car. Just up ahead. That's them.'

Macleod started to walk quicker, but then the woman looking at him suddenly showed a face of pain and anguish. Looking down below her neck, Macleod could see a dagger had just been plunged into her and red was starting to stain the top she was wearing. Ross come up from the other side, approaching the driver. As he did, the door opened, catching him in the knees. It was then pulled back and pushed at him again, hitting him on the head and he fell to the ground. A woman emerged from the car with a bag over her shoulder and began to run.

'Hope,' shouted Macleod. 'Stop her.'

Hope took off from the other line of cars, weaving away between the two lines before sprinting after the woman. Meanwhile, Macleod had opened the car door where the woman was struggling with the dagger. She'd pulled it halfway out, but it tumbled from her hands and Macleod pressed both of his onto the wound. Blood was pouring over his hand, and he was struggling to contain the flow.

'Get me a medic. Paramedic,' shouted Macleod. He looked

along the line and saw an ambulance at the rear.

'Somebody get that ambulance down here; get me a paramedic.'

As the blood poured over him, Zoe Jillings looked directly at him.

'She said . . .' and then the woman's voice was lost as she breathed deep, but with a hard gasp to it, as she struggled to take in air, maybe due to fluid on the lungs. Macleod was no expert. He didn't know. All he was doing was pressing down hard on the wound, trying to stop the blood from coming out.

'Loved me, loved me.' Then there was no more.

A man put a hand on Macleod's shoulder and pulled him away from the car. The green-suited man stepped in front of Macleod, and he saw the man begin to work on Zoe Jillings. Macleod looked over the car and saw Ross getting groggily to his feet.

'You okay?'

'Not really. It's a hell of a bump. What the heck happened to her,' said Ross, looking at the passenger side of the car.

Macleod wasn't listening though. He swung round to see a hard-running Hope, following a woman with a bag that was too big to carry. They were running towards a smaller pier, further up. Macleod saw Julia Fluke getting taken off her feet by Hope in what resembled a rugby tackle. Both women tumbled off the edge of the small pier and disappeared into the water beyond.

Macleod ran around the car. 'Stay here,' he said to Ross. 'Give that paramedic help if he needs it.'

Ross didn't look like he was able to give anybody help and merely collapsed on his backside onto the bonnet of the car, but Macleod couldn't wait. He ran as hard as he could, away from the line of cars, down along the shore onto the small pier.

As he looked over the edge, he could see his colleague holding someone by the collar, lifting her out of the water. Slowly Hope was making her way in. As they got to the shore, Julia Fluke tried to struggle, but Hope threw her down onto the stones. She knelt on her back, put her hands up behind and slapped some handcuffs on the woman's wrists. Macleod stood beside as Hope cautioned her and then stood up breathing heavily.

'It's bloody cold in there,' she said. 'I wasn't looking for an early morning swim.'

'Where's the money?' asked Macleod. Hope turned to look back at the water and saw a man kayaking along. He was picking up a black bag, and he pulled it on board the kayak. Macleod watched him pull the zip back. The next minute he was waving money in the air.

'You dancer, you absolute dancer,' the man was shouting into the air. 'This is it. Barbados, here we come.'

Macleod laughed, looked over at Hope. 'I'll go disappoint the man. Go back up to Ross. I think he took a heck of a bang in the head. I'm sure some uniform can take this one away. Going to be a long morning, interviews and that. You should probably get checked out.'

'I'm all right,' said Hope. 'I'm all right. I just want to see you talk to that guy about the money.'

Macleod strode over, waving his badge in the air. He gave a beckoning hand to the man in the kayak. As it reached shore, Macleod asked for the money, and he saw the man's disappointed face.

'Don't I get a finder's fee?' the man asked.

Macleod shook his head. 'I'll tell you what, though, if you come up to Tobermory Police Station, I'll buy you a coffee.'

The man shook his head. 'That's the trouble with you police these days. You don't know how to live a little. Pair of us could have gone our own ways with this stuff.' Macleod was about to chastise the man, but he looked around and saw a dripping wet Hope still watching. He picked up the bag and started making his way towards her.

'We've done it, and we've saved an innocent man,' said Hope with a smile.

Macleod suddenly stopped walking. 'Yes, but there wasn't much innocent about Curtis James.'

Chapter 25

Macleod stood in the tower, watching the arrival of an aircraft with Harold Lyme in front of him. Harold had been explaining about how the aircraft had picked up the localiser but wasn't following the glide path signal and therefore was using the chart to come down to a certain height. They'd have to recognise the runway, identify clear markings on it before making further approach.

Macleod had no idea what the man was talking about, but he seemed to be enjoying telling him, so he just nodded. Behind him, Kylie Youngs was talking to Hope about the detail of her daily work. Macleod could tell that Hope was just giving it the customary lip service that said, 'I'm a police officer. Of course, I'm interested.' In truth, the job was done, and they were just killing time before getting the ferry back over.

Sure, there'd be more reports. The two killers were being transported over to the mainland. The money had also been picked up and taken away by a secure load. Earlier in the day, Clarissa had arrived, having flown back from her dealings in Blackpool, and she'd gone straight to sleep, grabbing a couple of hours before they were going to return on the ferry. When she arrived, she seemed quite annoyed that nobody had informed her they'd just about wrapped up.

Macleod thanked Harold and started to make his way downstairs, but he saw Curtis James coming up the spiral staircase. Macleod stepped aside as the airport manager thumped his way up the steps announcing his arrival. He pulled up his trousers by the belt in an action that Macleod thought ridiculous. If your clothing was that difficult to manage, you should get a better belt.

He watched the man sheepishly look away from Hope, but then give an excited glance towards Kylie. The young girl turned, and she smiled. Macleod realised that she did this with all men. In fact, with most people. It just seemed that Curtis interpreted it slightly differently. Then again, he thought Curtis could interpret anything as a pass at him.

'That's us just about wrapped up, Mr James. I hope the closing of the airport earlier on wasn't too inconvenient for you.'

'Of course not, Inspector. I take it that some of those things are going to remain . . .'

'I don't think they'll remain that quiet,' said Macleod. 'When this goes to court, I can imagine that a fair number of details will come out, especially about the container.'

Curtis waved his hands as if to shush Macleod. 'I don't think we need to go into that here.'

'The container,' said Kylie from behind him. 'Everyone knows about the container. Your guys were down with it opened; it all had circus stuff in it. They said that was yours, Curtis, at least that's the rumour going round.'

Curtis's face fell and Harold, having seen the aircraft touch down, spun round in his seat.

'I never knew you were into the circus,' he said politely,

but he threw a glance to Kylie, who then erupted, burst out laughing. Curtis turned and stomped his way back down the stairs.

'I think there's going to be a lot come out,' said Macleod, 'when the case goes to court. Things I can't talk about now. I do hope you'll all be okay here. It's not easy when you've been working with someone who turns out to have been a murderer.'

'It was Julia that killed Eppy?' asked Harold. 'All because . . .'

'All because,' said Macleod, 'he'd begun to spot the ferry flights coming through, begun to spot the operator. He asked the question, that's what she told us anyway, and she couldn't take the risk. She thought about Mr James, certain things she knew about him allowed her to set him up. He'd have taken the fall as well if we hadn't worked out what was going on. It was a good trap. The man was too stupid to get out of it as well. He wasn't like you, Mr Lyme, straight up. Or you, Miss Youngs. For all that I find your lifestyle not to my taste, you didn't lie to me. You were upfront with it, and for that, I thank you both.'

'You're not bad for a bit of a fuddy-duddy,' said Kylie.

'Fuddy-duddy?' said Macleod. 'I didn't think that was a word that you would come up with.'

'Oh no. That's what she said,' said Kylie, pointing at Hope. 'Said you were a good one, despite being a fuddy-duddy.'

'Just smoothing along investigations,' said Hope. Then she turned away, not able to look at Macleod.

'Regardless, thank you both. I hope not to see you again in my professional capacity.'

As he descended the stairs, he could hear Hope chastising Kylie for getting her into trouble. But it wasn't as if he didn't know. Amongst the team, he was the older one. After all, he didn't have that dynamic ability that Clarissa had. Earlier on in the day, he'd received a phone call from one of the inspectors at Blackpool Police Station. Apparently, Clarissa had run rings around his snatch team and apprehended both subjects that the team were meant to be going for. He was particularly impressed by the way she'd smacked the door into a suspect and said, when he looked at her, he couldn't believe the ferocity inside the woman.

Macleod had smiled at that one. Not many knew Clarissa the way she was, dogged, determined, and generally not giving much of a toss anymore. He liked that about age. Sometimes you got to a point where you just thought, *Who cares? What's the worst that can happen?* He learned that as he went along; there were times when what was the worst that could happen? Generally, when he showed up, it already had.

Jona had confirmed earlier on in the day that Julia's hand size was rather large for a woman and matched the impressions made on John Epson, while Zoe Jillings had a hand size that matched those on Sarah Pullet. Sarah had been unfortunate. It turned out that she had found the drugs when cleaning the toilets. It seemed that Frauke Haas would come in, go to the toilet, leave the drugs in the cistern, and then either Zoe or Julia would pop down, pick up whatever packet was there, and take it home.

Zoe had been brought in due to meeting Julia and started having an affair with her. Unfortunately, when they went to run, Julia's real intention, to have a stooge who could do a lot of the drug work and possibly get all the blame dumped onto them, had come to the fore. Fortunately, the paramedic had done a better job than Macleod had of dealing with Zoe's wounds. He did comment that the pressure the Inspector had kept on the victim had kept her alive. The good side about Zoe having been knifed was she was more than happy to dump Julia right in it.

Macleod walked across to the gate that separated the airside from the landside, and opening it, he saw a green car pulling into the carpark. The horn beeped, and he watched a woman with gaudy trousers and a brightly coloured shawl flung around her, make her way over. He hadn't seen her since her arrival. Instead of reporting to him, as soon as Clarissa had heard she wasn't actually required, she told Hope she was going to bed. Apparently, there'd been a few swear words about Macleod sending her off to Blackpool.

As Clarissa approached, Macleod put out his hand. She took it and he shook it in a strong fashion.

'Well done,' he said. 'I received a call this morning. One of the inspectors down at Blackpool Police Station said you taught their boys a few things.'

'You sent me down to Blackpool. I hadn't slept.'

'Did you not hear me?' said Macleod. 'I said, well done.'

'Seoras, do you know what age I am? You could've sent Ross down.'

'But then we wouldn't have our drug runner. Ross couldn't have pulled that one off. They said you were waiting at the rear of a nightclub door but somehow accidentally closed it as she tried to come out of it. You also tackled her boyfriend.'

'In fairness, he wasn't her boyfriend, just somebody she picked up. You could probably throw a better punch than him.'

Macleod raised his eyes. 'Regardless, well done. I mean that. I might put you in for some sort of recognition, an award or that.'

'Now you're soft-soaping me, Seoras. Don't send me off like that. It was the middle of the night. I had to go into one of those nightclubs. Have you ever been in there with the music? It's deafening. You've got all these people running around as if they're in Ibiza, looking at me as if I'm their grandmother. I'm sure some of them shouldn't have been in there either. Did I ever tell you I used to do antiques? I used to actually solve crime around really nice people who served you tea and cakes. There used to be a bit of class to what I did. Now, I'm the only bit of class on this operation.'

Macleod raised a finger. 'Enough. It wasn't the class I sent down there that was coming to the fore.'

'Of course, it was class. It might've been old school, but it was class.'

Hope appeared over Macleod's shoulder. Then she gave a nod to Clarissa. 'He's actually impressed by what you did.'

'He's grovelling, is what he's doing,' said Clarissa. 'He's trying to apologise, without actually apologising, for sending me all the way to Blackpool.'

'Anyway, we need to get on the ferry,' said Macleod. 'Where's the car, Hope?'

'Oh, no, you're coming with me,' said Clarissa.

Macleod looked at Hope, shaking his head. 'Where's your car, Sergeant McGrath?'

'Ross packed it today with someone else's equipment. No seats left,' said Hope, smiling. 'Besides, you want to take a few fighting tips from this one.' Macleod stared at Hope as she walked off.

'Come on then, boss,' said Clarissa; 'time to get down to the ferry. Oh, by the way, they told me you stuck your hand in a load of blood. That right?'

'I thought I was Lady Macbeth trying to get rid of it afterwards. Everywhere. But she survived, so I guess it was the right thing to do.'

'Just tell me one thing, one thing,' said Clarissa. 'Does your mind work like that Curtis guy?'

'No,' said Macleod. 'Of course, it doesn't.'

'I don't think so,' said Clarissa. 'He barely batted an eyelid at me. Just looking at that young thing up in the tower all the time. That's not you. You appreciate a more mature woman.' Macleod cast a glance at Clarissa. She was laughing at his face. 'What's the matter?' she said. 'I know you're impressed by me.'

Macleod stopped as they got to the car. 'Did you hear what they said to me this morning? When he told me about how you handled yourself and what you did?'

'That they had a wild one down in Blackpool,' said Clarissa.

'Of sorts. Macleod's Rottweiler is what they said. It looks like my name's got out of Inverness.'

'Well,' said Clarissa, 'when you get a name like that, there's only one thing you can do, and that's own it. So, get your bottom in the car, Seoras. You should really learn to be a little bit more eccentric.'

Macleod shook his head, sat down in the green car, and then found his hair being swept away as Clarissa drove at pace from the carpark.

'Next time, I'm flying,' he said.

Read on to discover the Patrick
Smythe series!

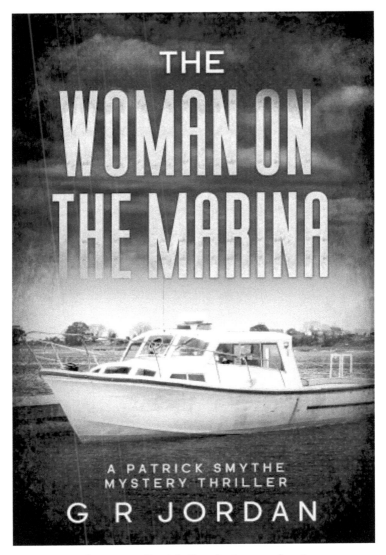

Start your Patrick Smythe journey here!

Patrick Smythe is a former Northern Irish policeman who

after suffering an amputation after a bomb blast, takes to the sea between the west coast of Scotland and his homeland to ply his trade as a private investigator. Join Paddy as he tries to work to his own ethics while knowing how to bend the rules he once enforced. Working from his beloved motorboat 'Craigantlet', Paddy decides to rescue a drug mule in this short story from the pen of G R Jordan.

Join G R Jordan's monthly newsletter about forthcoming releases and special writings for his tribe of avid readers and then receive your free Patrick Smythe short story.

Go to https://bit.ly/PatrickSmythe for your Patrick Smythe journey to start!

About the Author

GR Jordan is a self-published author who finally decided at forty that in order to have an enjoyable lifestyle, his creative beast within would have to be unleashed. His books mirror that conflict in life where acts of decency contend with self-promotion, goodness stares in horror at evil, and kindness blindsides us when we at our worst. Corrupting our world with his parade of wondrous and horrific characters, he highlights everyday tensions with fresh eyes whilst taking his methodical, intelligent mainstays on a roller-coaster ride of dilemmas, all the while suffering the banter of their provocative sidekicks.

A graduate of Loughborough University where he masqueraded as a chemical engineer but ultimately played American football, Gary had worked at changing the shape of cereal flakes and pulled a pallet truck for a living. Watching vegetables freeze at -40'C was another career highlight and he was also one of the Scottish Highlands "blind" air traffic controllers.

These days he has graduated to answering a telephone to people in trouble before telephoning other people to sort it out.

Having flirted with most places in the UK, he is now based in the Isle of Lewis in Scotland where his free time is spent between raising a young family with his wife, writing, figuring out how to work a loom and caring for a small flock of chickens. Luckily, his writing is influenced by his varied work and life experience as the chickens have not been the poetical inspiration he had hoped for!

You can connect with me on:

🌐 https://grjordan.com

📘 https://facebook.com/carpetlessleprechaun

Subscribe to my newsletter:

✉ https://bit.ly/PatrickSmythe

Also by G R Jordan

G R Jordan writes across multiple genres including crime, dark and action adventure fantasy, feel good fantasy, mystery thriller and horror fantasy. Below is a selection of his work. Whilst all books are available across online stores, signed copies are available at his personal shop.

Man Overboard! (Highlands & Islands Detective Book 19)
https://grjordan.com/product/man-overboard
A Coastguard's nightmare repeats. The fledgling tourist season is in tatters. Can Macleod and McGrath find the killer amongst the hordes of holidaymakers?

When the Coastguard note an increase in drownings from travellers falling overboard from passenger vessels, Macleod is called in to satisfy an itch that these may not be innocent accidents. When the victims are all found to be from troubled marriages, the team must seek the hidden orchestrator of spring mayhem. Can Seoras and Hope find the killer before widow maker of the seas strikes again?

To jump or not to jump, sometimes it's not a choice!

The Execution of Celebrity (A Kirsten Stewart Thriller #6)
https://grjordan.com/product/the-execution-of-celebrity
Television personalities suddenly disappear. A confluence of agents in the North of Scotland. Can Kirsten Stewart make the connection and prevent an on-air execution.

When Scottish celebrities begin to disappear, the police enlist the help of the Service to find the guilty parties. But Kirsten and her team are stretched as a flood of foreign agents seem to be massing in the Scottish Highlands. Can the team make the connection and stop a broadcast that will leave every citizen numb to their core?

Sometimes there is such a thing as bad publicity!

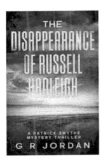

The Disappearance of Russell Hadleigh (Patrick Smythe Book 1)
https://grjordan.com/product/the-disappearance-of-russell-hadleigh
A retired judge fails to meet his golf partner. His wife calls for help while running a fantasy play ring. When Russians start co-opting into a fairly-traded clothing brand, can Paddy untangle the strands before the bodies start littering the golf course?

In his first full novel, Patrick Smythe, the single-armed former policeman, must infiltrate the golfing social scene to discover the fate of his client's husband. Assisted by a young starlet of the greens, Paddy tries to understand just who bears a grudge and who likes to play in the rough, culminating in a high stakes showdown where lives are hanging by the reaction of a moment. If you love pacey action, suspicious motives and devious characters, then Paddy Smythe operates amongst your kind of people.

Love is a matter of taste but money always demands more of its suitor.

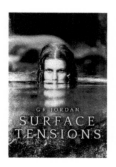

Surface Tensions (Island Adventures Book 1)
https://grjordan.com/product/surface-tensions
Mermaids sighted near a Scottish island. A town exploding in anger and distrust. And Donald's got to get the sexiest fish in town, back in the water.

"Surface Tensions" is the first story in a series of Island adventures from the pen of G R Jordan. If you love comic moments, cosy adventures and light fantasy action, then you'll love these tales with a twist. Get the book that amazon readers said, "perfectly captures life in the Scottish Hebrides" and that explores "human nature at its best and worst".

Something's stirring the water!

Corpse Reviver (A Contessa Munroe Mystery #1)
https://grjordan.com/product/corspe-reviver
A widowed Contessa flees to the northern waters in search of adventure. An entrepreneur dies on an ice pack excursion. But when the victim starts moonlighting from his locked cabin, can the Contessa uncover the true mystery of his death?

Catriona Cullodena Munroe, widow of the late Count de Los Palermo, has fled the family home, avoiding the scramble for title and land. As she searches for the life she always wanted, the Contessa, in the company of the autistic and rejected Tiff, must solve the mystery of a man who just won't let his business go.

Corpse Reviver is the first murder mystery involving the formidable and sometimes downright rude lady of leisure and her straight talking niece. Bonded by blood, and thrown together by fate, join this pair of thrill seekers as they realise that flirting with danger brings a price to pay.

Milton Keynes UK
Ingram Content Group UK Ltd.
UKHW022109220424
441558UK00001BA/13